LYNNE STEWART

TRACKING HIS TRUE MATE

BOOK ONE IN THE
TRUE MATE SHIFTER SERIES

For the readers.
Thanks for making writing fun.

Chapter 1

His eyes were like piercing blue daggers, and they drew me in instantly, so fast that I had almost forgotten how to speak. Even now, a flutter of excitement stirred in my belly as I thought of the hunky shifter who had appeared at the circulation desk that morning. I had all but melted on the spot when his eyes raked over my body. It had taken every ounce of my self-control not to lead him directly to the lady's bathroom when he licked his lips and asked about my plans for this evening. Any existing plans wouldn't have mattered; I would have cleared my entire week for him if he wanted me to.

I took the stairs two at a time, hoping to avoid seeing Ella on my way out the door, but I had no such luck. My sister was curled up on the sofa, reading and sipping a cup of coffee.

Probably decaf, I thought. Caffeinated beverages after lunch were a little too wild and crazy for her.

"So, you're going out *again* tonight," she said, looking up from her page and emphasizing the word 'again' in a sarcastic way. I tried to ignore her tone, but her disapproval stung.

"Yes. I met someone at work, and he's taking me out to

dinner."

She rolled her eyes. "Does Lance know about this new friend? Or Patrick?"

I frowned. "I'm not exclusive with Lance or Patrick. They know I see other people. Hell, they're probably both on a date right now." Honestly, I had no idea what they were doing tonight. Not because I didn't care, but because whatever they did with someone else really wasn't any of my business.

My answer did little to satisfy Ella, and she narrowed her eyes at me. She was never shy about sharing her views on my love life. Like most other shifters, she believed that werewolves should remain celibate until finding their true mate or at least until they were locked into a regular mating bond, but I didn't see it that way. My sister, fifteen years my senior, was living proof of how archaic that belief was. At thirty-six, she was still waiting for him to materialize. And while she waited and hoped each day that her perfect match would find her, I spent my time praying to never be found.

There was nothing more to say; neither of us was going to be convinced by the other, so I said good night to her and walked to my car alone. Outside, the house was quiet. The only noise came from the wind moving through the leaves high in the trees.

She isn't wrong. We should wait for our mate, too. My wolf was just as huffy as my sister. The difference was that once we had a horny male shifter in front of us, her feelings changed considerably. I sent a mental picture to her, a memory of our last tryst. The image was enough to stifle her objections.

I shivered, in part because of the cold, but also from

thinking about how good it had felt to writhe underneath the strong male. He wasn't my first conquest, either. Patrick had been the first and I would always be grateful for that.

He had been nervous when we first decided to have sex as teenagers, worried that by taking my virginity, he was robbing me of something special. Something sacred. But that was utter nonsense, and I had told him as much. Even if I had a true mate somewhere, he didn't own my body. *At least not yet*, I corrected myself.

With a bond in place, I would never be allowed to be with another man again. Male werewolves were notorious for being possessive of their mates, often forbidding them from even engaging in friendships with the opposite sex. The fact that I had male friends and that I had slept with some of them over the past three years was likely more than any true mate would be willing to deal with. Add that to all the other ways females were expected to be submissive to their men, and it became clear why I had no desire to ever go down that route.

So, while my sister and every other female I knew dreamt of the day she would meet her true mate, I wanted to avoid it for as long as possible. My friendships and my freedom meant more than experiencing a strong connection with some random control freak.

I cranked the engine of my old truck, thankful that it didn't put up a fuss as I backed out of the drive. I would have to replace it with a new car at some point but getting rid of Dad's truck felt wrong. He had been so excited to bring it home and had taken excellent care of it for years until Mom died. Once she was gone, things like caring for the family had fallen squarely on Ella's shoulders.

I blinked away the tears, instantly annoyed. Who thinks about their dead parents on the way to a night of deviant sex? Maybe I was just nervous. I might not be a virgin, but this was the first time I was going out on a date to meet a stranger. Patrick, Lance, and the handful of other men I had been with were all trusted friends.

We should go home, my wolf whined. We had both been distracted by the handsome stranger, but now that he wasn't looking at her with those enticing blue eyes, she was having second thoughts. I chewed on my lip and toyed with the idea of calling Patrick. But wouldn't that cross some kind of boundary? To ask him what I should do about going on a date with another man?

No, I decided finally. Patrick was a good friend. He would tell me if going on the date was dumb. I quickly dialed his number, happy when he answered on the second ring.

"Hey, Mariam," he said, breathing hard into his phone. "What's up?"

My cheeks flamed. His voice had a sexy hitch to it. "Um…I have a question for you, but if you're…busy… I can talk to you another time."

He chuckled, instantly knowing what my hesitation was implying. "I just finished a workout at the gym. What do you need?"

"Oh, okay," I answered, hating the relief I felt that he wasn't with another girl. *What happened to no strings attached?* I chided myself. "I have a date tonight with a guy I met at the library. He seems…experienced, and I just wanted to know if I was being stupid about meeting him, you know? He isn't from our pack. I don't really know anything about him."

There was a long pause on the other end. I thought that maybe the call was dropped until Patrick gave a long sigh. "Is this about sex, Mare? You know I can take care of you if you just want to meet him because you're horny."

My heart pounded harder in my chest. "It's not just that. I think I might like him. Is that so wrong?" The question hung in the air, echoing in the silence.

We had agreed to have an open arrangement before sleeping together. That way, we could both retain our freedom, and even if our sexual relationship ended, we could keep our friendship.

Patrick knew that I took advantage of that freedom with some other males, but that knowledge came with some strain on his end. Even without being his mate, the territorial pull for male werewolves was hard to overcome.

If only the sex hadn't been so good, we might have stopped after just the one time and spared him the emotional flare-ups. But countless orgasms later, we both still wanted more.

"Of course not," Patrick ground out, his teeth clenched. "I don't own you, Mariam. I just don't want you to get hurt by someone who might be using you."

Everything he said was true, but the edge in his voice told me that he was also trying to control his own possessiveness. Calling him about this had been a mistake.

"Okay, thanks, Patrick. I'll talk to you later. Have a good night." I rushed to end the call, ignoring the growl he gave from being cut off. In addition to being possessive, his wolf sometimes got it in his head that he had the right to punish me for stupid shit like that. But that's just another danger of sleeping with a werewolf; they all wanted to become an authority in your life.

The restaurant was oddly empty for a Friday night, with only a few cars parked outside. I spotted an expensive-looking SUV, guessing instantly that the handsome stranger was also probably wealthy. He projected the confidence of someone who could do anything he wanted, which was a little off-putting.

Ignoring my wolf's whine, I walked up the steps and through the front door that was held open for me. While our pack had sufficient funds to care for all its members, Dark Claw was not a wealthy pack like some others in the area. This was the fanciest restaurant on our lands, a place that I had never visited and was typically only used for special occasions. With about two thousand wolves, there were always more than a few anniversaries or pregnancies or birthdays being celebrated on a given weekend. It definitely wasn't a place where a broke library assistant went for dinner.

I picked up his scent right away; it was warm, sweet, and intoxicating, like spiced rum. He must have scented me, too, because soon he was walking toward me from where he was waiting at the bar.

"After I left, I realized my error in not getting your name," he growled near my ear as he enveloped me in a hug. It was a polite greeting at first, but the deep tenor of his voice and the feeling of his arms around me created a pulse between my legs, and I felt the warmth of my need spread.

I blushed at my own reaction, knowing that he would easily be able to smell my arousal. His nostrils flared when we pulled apart, his grin showing elongated fangs. I cleared my throat, expecting my voice to crack. "I'm Mariam. And you are?"

"Alexander," he replied, grabbing his glass from the bar, and guiding me to a nearby table. A waiter was already hovering nearby. "What would you like to drink, Mariam?"

"Wine would be great. White, please." I didn't know much about alcohol, but white wine seemed to taste better than red. Alexander nodded as the waiter made the note and left. I looked around the room. It wasn't completely empty, but there were only a few other patrons. The pack's alpha, Jeremy, raised an eyebrow at me from a booth in the corner.

I dropped my gaze, suddenly self-conscious. I knew there had been whispers in the pack about my decision to not remain a virgin but being out with a male and making no mating announcement was basically advertising that I was a whore.

I gritted my teeth at the word, triggering myself with the thought. Somehow, being a sex-positive female meant that I was a whore in the eyes of my pack, but I refused to believe it for myself.

Alexander regarded me with interest, noticing my change in demeanor as his eyes flickered to Jeremy. "Your alpha doesn't approve of you dating?"

I smiled at his bold question. "We don't usually date in my pack. Wolves stay single until their true mate presents himself or until they enter into a mating agreement with someone else if they don't want to wait."

"That's very conservative of them. But you have decided to go on a date with me tonight anyway," he said, leaning in with a curious twinkle in his eye. "Am I your first date, Mariam?"

Another bold question. I was beginning to like Alexander. "No in some ways, yes in others. This is absolutely my first time having dinner at this restaurant."

"Good. Hopefully you enjoy it," Alexander said, leaning back in his chair. I wasn't sure if the answer I gave was what he was hoping for. His expression gave nothing away.

"I'm sure it will be wonderful," I said with a smile. And truthfully, the food was delicious. Alexander was good company, and he kept me entertained with stories from his travels. He worked as a consultant and was visiting my pack to have a meeting with Jeremy and his beta the following day. He was only in town a short time before returning to his pack for a much-needed break from work.

"I'm staying at the Feldman," he said, glancing at me discreetly. Part of me wondered if he was just saying that to test my reaction. Would I storm out, offended by the innuendo, or would I stay and talk about his hotel?

Of course, I chose to stay.

"I've heard that's a nice place," I said casually. My tone caused him to smile wider, this time showing a dimple on one side. Once again, I was lost in his eyes.

"Would you like to see for yourself?" His offer was little more than a growl.

In the corner, I saw Jeremy stiffen, and I wanted to hide under the table. The last thing I needed was for the pack's alpha to be privy to my sex life, especially when it was so clear that he disapproved of sex outside of a mating bond. I snuck another look at him, only to panic as he stood and approached our table.

"Mr. Simon," Jeremy said, extending his hand to Alexander. "It's been a while."

Alexander gave him a smile in contrast to Jeremy's stern glare. "It is good to see you again, alpha. I was just getting to know a member of your pack better. Mariam has been very welcoming."

Jeremy's eyes flashed with anger, and my blush deepened and spread. I pushed my chair out to stand, but my alpha placed his hand on my shoulder.

"I'll make this simple for you, Alexander. I was looking forward to our meeting tomorrow, but I think it is best that you leave this evening. Please go and collect your things from your hotel room."

Alexander chuckled and placed some cash on the table. His demeanor was unbothered, but an alpha telling a wolf to leave their territory was serious. He had no option but to go if he wanted to keep his life.

"That's a shame. Maybe another time, Mariam?" He leaned forward to tuck a lock of hair behind my ear. His finger traced my face, falling short of touching my neck when Jeremy bared his teeth.

Alexander held his hands up in mock surrender, his eyes sparkling with humor. He swaggered out the door without looking back.

I ventured a glance up to look at Jeremy. His jaw ticked, betraying his anger, so my eyes returned to the ground. As much as I wanted to believe that I didn't care what people said about me, what the alpha thought was the one thing that did matter. He had the power to isolate or exile members. I heard from Ella that he even had the ability to require wolves within the pack to mate, which was why I tried to avoid him like the plague. Jeremy could be within his right to bind us together, breaking any true mate bond that might exist for us with others. At least, that's what my sister told me.

"Let's go," Jeremy growled, helping me to my feet and steering me back to his table. My wolf was alert, knowing instinctually that our alpha was not pleased with us. The emotions warring within her spilled over into me. I tried to soothe her, but I had no idea what was going to happen.

Chapter 2

"What am I going to do with you, Mariam?" Jeremy ran his fingers through his hair, an exasperated look on his face. Although he was only in his mid-thirties, the responsibilities of being an alpha had already begun to age him. There was silver in his hair where there had only been black a few years earlier. Without a mate, the whole weight of the job fell on his shoulders, and I felt a little guilty for adding to his burden.

His eyes flashed when I didn't answer or apologize. "There is a proper way to do things, to live, Mariam. Have you no shame? Running around our pack, fucking anything that will move? What will your true mate think when he learns what you've been doing?"

My anger boiled, giving me unnatural courage. "I don't care what he thinks. I don't want a true mate."

Jeremy's eyes widened at my words, his face torn between anger at my outburst and confusion over what I had said. He probably assumed that I was as eager as every other member in our pack to find my other half.

"And why is that, Mariam? Obviously, you're not

apprehensive about sex. Is it the biting that concerns you?"

I forced myself not to show my embarrassment over his taunting. "Not every female wants to be owned by a male, alpha."

Understanding dawned on him, causing him to scowl. "You prefer to run wild rather than being controlled."

Yup. That was about the size of it. But I wasn't going to say that aloud. It didn't matter anyway; my silence was as good as an agreement.

"Do you realize how tempting it is to just assign you to another wolf, right here, right now?" Jeremy hissed. "I could give you to someone who would have no problem straightening you out. He'd probably even relish the task of whipping your ass into shape."

My face paled. If we were in wolf form, my animal would have already been on her back, showing him her belly in submission.

Jeremy smiled as if reading my mind. He wanted order in our pack and assigning me to a bull-headed asshole would ensure that order reigned. "Consider this your only warning, Mariam. Start acting like a proper she-wolf, or you will find yourself mated before the next full moon."

He tilted his head to the door, indicating that I was free to go.

I was fuming on the drive back home when I suddenly changed direction and veered toward the Feldman Hotel.

The doorman looked surprised to see me but didn't comment when I stepped inside. I stood awkwardly in the lobby, realizing I didn't have Alexander's phone number or any way to let him know I was at his hotel. If he hadn't already left, that is.

You should listen to our alpha. My wolf's warning came with some reproach. It was very black and white for her: the alpha told us to keep it in our pants, so there was no reason for me to be standing in a hotel lobby.

I tried to reason with her and remind her that she hated the idea of being mated as much as I did. If our alpha really cared for us, he wouldn't be threatening to force us into anything like that.

She whined again, pacing uncomfortably in my mind. I needed to shift soon and let her have some time to run. Part of being a werewolf was learning to respect the balance between us. She refrained from taking over my humanity and forcing a shift, and I needed to make sure she felt heard and had a chance to run. It was a hierarchical relationship, with me being the dominant partner.

"Mariam?" Alexander's voice tore me away from my thoughts. He leaned against an ornate pillar next to the elevator, his gaze sweeping over me.

I took a deep breath and closed the distance between us, bringing my lips to his when we collided. His hands found my back, waist, and ass, rubbing and touching everywhere at once, setting my skin on fire. I tore my mouth away and met his eyes. "Are you leaving or something? Did I come at a bad time?"

His chuckle vibrated deep in his chest. "Not at all, Mariam." He pushed the elevator button to take us upstairs. Suddenly self-conscious about our public display, I glanced around hastily. The receptionist glared at us with her lips drawn tight. She was a member of my pack, but I couldn't remember her name. I gulped. Hopefully, she wouldn't contact our alpha about my indiscretion. The doorman looked less interested. He had pulled out his phone, focusing his attention elsewhere.

Alexander steered me inside the elevator when the doors opened and immediately covered my body again with his. The pressure of his erection rubbed against me, causing me to forget about the receptionist entirely.

My wolf groaned with me, content to push back against his bulge. Alexander's hand found my face, turning my lips to his. He began devouring my mouth, nipping, tasting, and feasting on me like he was a starving man.

We couldn't make it to the room fast enough; he started removing his tie and jacket before we even closed the door. I inhaled his scent, and my fangs elongated to reflect my arousal.

If we intended to mate, he would need to bite me on the base of my neck, so elongated fangs were just part of getting turned on, especially for males. Of course, neither Alexander nor I wanted to mate, so he had to be careful and not accidentally latch on. I wasn't under the same kind of pressure; my wolf just rose to the surface to experience some of the fun, too.

Alexander's eyes changed again, showing the wolf just under the surface. He reached around to unzip my dress, and I started removing his shirt. My fingers stretched across his chest, enjoying the way his muscles felt under them.

Alexander didn't appear to notice as he snapped the clasp on my bra and dipped his head to catch one of my breasts in his mouth. I leaned back and moaned, amazed at how skilled he was at stimulating my nipple. His hand found my other tit, squeezing and testing the weight in his palm.

He pushed forward, guiding me to the bed. I ran my hands through his hair, no longer caring what Jeremy thought. This was what I wanted. This was what I *needed*.

Hours later, after making love in several different locations around the room, I collected my scattered clothing with a satisfied smile. He reclined in the bed, enjoying the view of my partial undress.

"You are the first shifter woman I've ever fucked," he admitted, lighting a cigarette, and inhaling deeply. I wrinkled my nose against the strong smell, thankful to be leaving soon. "All the others were humans, and I think you've ruined them for me."

I had never slept with a human, so I had nothing to compare it with. Was there really that much of a difference? "All my partners have been other shifters, but it was good for me, too."

His eyes clouded over for a minute, trying to suppress his jealousy over the idea of me sleeping with other wolves. The same look of concentration had crossed his face when he climaxed inside of me and had to force himself not to bite my neck in the heat of passion. The man in him understood that this was a one-night stand, but his wolf would be upset that the female he had just fucked wasn't his to claim. My wolf was smug about being his only shifter conquest, but even she was a little uncomfortable knowing that there were human women he had bedded before us.

I sighed, wanting to chastise her for that ridiculous line of thinking, but it wouldn't do any good. As much as I had enjoyed the casual fling, my wolf was built for monogamy. She wanted to stay and make the whole thing permanent.

She went through the same rollercoaster of emotions whenever it was time for us to leave.

"I hope I didn't get you in trouble with your alpha," Alexander offered when he had his wolf back under control. His gaze dipped to the round of my ass, and he reached for it, hesitating as he did so. "Do you think…before you go, I could…"

"No," I said firmly, already knowing what the question would be. He nodded and settled back in the bed, but his wolf was already showing again in his eyes.

The need to dispense domestic discipline was ingrained in werewolf males, and having sex seemed to bring out that desire in them all. A few times, I had let Patrick take me over his knee because he was on the verge of losing control of his wolf by holding back. As pleased as he was with his handiwork when he was done, I wasn't able to sit without wincing for days afterward.

At least Alexander was respectful and wasn't pressuring me to accept a spanking. It could be worse, that's for sure. A real mate probably wouldn't even ask first.

"If your alpha ever allows me back on your pack lands, I want to know how to contact you," he said, fiddling with the hotel bedding absentmindedly.

"I'm sure you'll be able to find me. Remember, I'm the girl from the library." I leaned down to kiss him again but stopped when he took another drag from his cigarette. The desire to taste his lips left as quickly as it came.

It was just as well. I needed to get home before it got too late, and Ella started to worry. Alexander offered to walk me back to my car, but I didn't want anyone else to see us together. I didn't want to press my luck any more than I already had.

Downstairs, I stepped off the elevator only to be assaulted by a new smell. This one put Alexander's scent to shame, and it stopped me in my tracks. It was cinnamon and rain and everything wonderful, all wrapped up together.

My heart hammered in my chest as I looked around, confused. The scent was nothing like I had ever experienced before. It definitely wasn't here when I arrived. Across the lobby, a tall man locked eyes with me, and a smile spread across his face. I frowned as he stalked toward me, closing the space between us in just a few strides.

He was gorgeous; that much was undeniable. His dark hair matched his eyes perfectly. His short beard was trimmed neatly against his chiseled face, highlighting his rustic features. His evening jacket settled comfortably across his broad shoulders in a way that said the suit was made for him. The men he was with nudged one another, watching him with interest as he made his way across the room.

My wolf perked up, her full attention on him. As he came closer, she started spinning and giving happy, playful yips. I stumbled backward when he leaned forward to inhale deeply, but he grabbed me before I could fall. Or, more likely, before I could turn and bolt.

"Mate." He growled low in his throat, and his eyes flashed intensely. "Why do you smell like another male?"

I swallowed hard and tried to shake him off, but his grip only tightened. "You're hurting me," I accused. "Let me go."

"I don't think so," he replied darkly. "Answer me." His snarl told me he was close to losing control of his wolf as he breathed in my scent again. Maybe I could use his lack of restraint in my favor.

"I smell like another male because I was just upstairs fucking one. He's still there now, in the bed we shared." The words ignited a fire in him, causing him to tear his hand away from me and rush to the stairwell without glancing back. The other wolves in his group were momentarily stunned. They looked at each other and then at me before following him upstairs.

I sent a silent apology to Alexander but didn't waste any time running back to the truck, knowing that this would be my only opportunity to get away. I had to put as much distance between myself and the male wolf as possible if I wanted to remain unmated.

I peeled out of the driveway, fumbling to dial Patrick as my truck swerved and straightened.

"Hello?" His voice sounded groggy, like I had woken him up. A glance at the clock said it was after one in the morning, so I probably had.

"Patrick? I need your help," I gulped, unsure how he would react to what I was going to tell him. "I was at the Feldman Hotel, and I think I saw my mate. My true mate."

That woke him up. Patrick growled. "Come to my place. We can talk about this when you get here."

Even though he couldn't see it through the phone, I nodded and hung up. Thoughts raced through my mind about what I would need to do. Once a male found his true mate, there was no getting rid of him without breaking the bond. Of course, most females were all too happy to be found and claimed, so there was no need to try to escape them. But in my case, the unrelenting pull he felt would ruin everything.

I struggled to keep my wolf under control as I drove. She wanted to run back to the handsome stranger and receive his bite. She was furious that I was taking her away from him. I tried to reason with her. *It would take all our freedom away. He would control our every move.*

We don't know that, she snapped back at me. *Maybe he will care for us and allow us to have our freedom.*

I snorted at her ignorance. The man had grabbed my arm to prevent me from leaving and was probably tearing apart a hotel room in a jealous rage at this very moment. There was no way he would be okay with an open relationship status.

I'm not okay with it either, just for the record. My wolf curled up in a corner, facing away from me and pouting. It was better than her trying to take control from me, so I let her be.

I arrived at Patrick's apartment a few minutes later, unsure of what I could do to prevent the male wolf from following my scent. I had some body splash in the glove compartment, so I sprayed it around the truck and left a few sprits as I walked to his door. Using the key Patrick had given me, I let myself in.

"Hello?" I called out as I wandered past the dark living room and kitchen, assuming he was still in the back bedroom. I was right; he was in bed, scrolling through his phone.

"Hey," he mumbled, setting it to the side.

"What are you looking at?" I asked curiously as I settled beside him in the bed. He started to wrap his arms around me before stiffening and moving away.

"Just trying to find something online to help." His voice was tight. "I smell him on you. And someone else...and sex."

Without warning, the sound of his bones shifting filled the room, and he tore through his shirt and boxer shorts. His wolf looked at me with longing and anger. I scooted off the bed, upset at myself for causing Patrick to lose control. I walked to the bathroom and turned on the shower before stripping off my clothes and laying them in a neat pile on the floor.

The hot water was soothing and helped calm my stiff muscles from the stressful night. I grabbed my shampoo from the rack, grateful that Patrick allowed me to stash some of my things at his place. I used his soap to scrub my entire body vigorously twice over.

When I was finally satisfied that there were no lingering smells on me, I stepped out of the shower and wrapped a large towel around my body. I padded across his bedroom to grab some extra clothes from his dresser.

Patrick was back in human form, but the wild look remained in his eyes. He was close to shifting again. He gave an appreciative groan when I dropped the towel and slipped into an oversized T-shirt. I could see in the mirror that his fangs were showing, and his erection was clearly outlined under his sheet.

He sighed with satisfaction when I returned to the bed, this time smelling only like myself and soap. His strong arms encircled me, careful not to touch me below the hem of the shirt. I frowned, knowing without a doubt that he was turned on by my near nudity. Any other night he would already be removing the last of my clothes and fingering me to my first orgasm. My own body reacted to that thought, inspiring me to rub suggestively against his hardness. I slowed to a stop when he didn't return the motion.

"Did you find out anything helpful about true mates?" I asked hesitantly, hoping that the topic wouldn't set him off again.

"I don't want to talk about this anymore tonight, Mare. The stuff on those sites probably isn't even accurate. Let's just get some sleep and deal with it in the morning."

I couldn't disagree with that. My body was exhausted, even though my mind was going a thousand miles a minute. What if the male werewolf tracked me to Patrick's apartment? And what happened at the hotel after I left? Surely someone would contact Jeremy if there was a huge scene, and that was something I'd have to deal with, too.

My breath caught in my chest, realizing that this was precisely what Jeremy hoped for. My true mate would do more than just keep me in line; with the bond complete, he'd be able to read my mind and anticipate my every move. And he would have every right to punish me as he saw fit.

There was only one option. Tomorrow I would leave the Dark Claw pack and the only family I had ever known.

Chapter 3

"You really think this is your only option?" Lance shoved his hands in his pockets and rocked back on his heels. Patrick had given him a stern look when he arrived but had calmed significantly when we made no attempt to touch each other. To be fair, Lance had sized him up the same way. Men.

Gossip was already spreading through the pack about my true mate being here. If Lance was correct, the male was going from house to house trying to find me. Ella had started texting me shortly after Patrick and I had woken up with the sunrise. She wouldn't understand my desire to run away from my mate, so there was no point in trying to explain it to her. All her messages went unread and unanswered.

"It's not forever, just until he leaves or gives up looking for me," I said, as much to myself as to Lance. I tried to reassure Patrick of the same thing, but he didn't seem convinced, either.

Lance set his jaw and crossed his arms. My eyes strayed to his bulging muscles. "Then I'm coming with you," he announced. "There isn't much for me here with the Dark Claw pack anyway. Maybe we could join another pack. Or start our own."

I rolled my eyes at his suggestion. Starting our own pack would be much more fun for a male shifter. They wouldn't have to conceive and birth the line of original members.

Patrick growled at the last comment because of the implication of sex. His arm found my shoulder and wrapped around it possessively. Lance's eyes narrowed at the sight, and he bared his teeth at Patrick.

"Enough," I said, shaking loose from Patrick's embrace. "I can't ask you to do that, Lance. I don't know when I'll be back or even where I'm going. Besides, if he finds me and you're there…."

Lance reached for me as I opened the truck door and pulled me to him, kissing me deeply and causing my heart to race. I didn't bother to finish the thought; we were all thinking the same thing. If he caught one of them with me, he would probably kill them on the spot and ask questions later.

Patrick wasted no time ripping Lance away, snarling as he grabbed his shirt by the collar. "She's mine," he fumed, the deep voice of his wolf speaking through him.

I stepped between them, trying to diffuse the situation and avoid bloodshed.

My intervention took some fire from Patrick's eyes, and he released Lance. Maybe some space would be best for the three of us and our friendship.

"Keep in touch and let me know how everything is going, okay?" I asked as I returned to the driver's side door. Neither man responded, both still eyeing each other suspiciously. I sighed and started the truck. Pulling away from Patrick's apartment felt different. I looked at the two male werewolves in the mirror, not knowing how long it would be before I saw them again.

I let out another deep breath as guilt flooded me. Against my better judgment, I turned left off his street and headed back home. Regardless of my differences with Ella, I still needed to say goodbye to her. I slowed to a stop in front of our childhood home, breathing in the familiar sight.

I forced myself to walk the stone path to the front door. Just as I was about to turn the handle, Ella swung the door open.

"Um… hi, Ella. I just need to pick up a few things." I contorted around her and slipped inside.

"Everyone in Dark Claw is talking about you," she whispered, turning to face me. "You have no idea the things they're saying. Is it true? Did you find your true mate?"

I held her gaze. "Yes," I answered evenly. "At least, I think so. I saw a wolf last night who said he was my mate. He smelled really good, and my wolf seemed to know him, so I guess he probably is."

Ella's eyes widened. "People are saying that you were at a hotel with another wolf and that he smelled someone else on you and that he…killed the wolf you were with, Mariam," she stammered.

My breath hitched. "He did *what*?" I had inadvertently sentenced Alexander to his death in my haste to get away. If I had stayed and calmed the crazy man in the lobby, maybe I would have been able to save him. I sank down onto the living room couch as the gravity of what happened hit me.

"Why would you do that? How could you be so stupid?" Ella hissed. "It was bad enough when you were sneaking around with those boys from school, but this was a wolf from another pack. When his family hears what happened, who knows what they will do. His alpha is going to blame us for his death, that's for sure."

Everything she said rang true; Alexander had been a guest on our lands. Jeremy would be held accountable for what happened, and he would hold me responsible for not obeying his orders.

As he should. This is our fault. My wolf shook with fear at the knowledge that we had let our alpha down and that he would be upset with us.

"I need to leave. *Now*," I said, my legs shaking as I stood again. Ella gave me a look of disbelief.

"Where are you going? You belong to this pack until your mate can claim you. And then you belong with him."

I shook my head. "I meant what I've always said, Ella. I'm not leaving with him. Not if I have anything to say about it."

I ran to my room and grabbed the suitcase from under my bed. I hastily began throwing clothes and cosmetics inside. The pressure was on even more now; I had to get out of Dark Claw boundaries before Jeremy found me. Or worse, my mate showed up.

My thoughts were interrupted by voices in the living room. The sweet smell from earlier at the hotel hit my nose, and my blood ran cold. *He's here!* My wolf shouted and did a happy spin in my mind's eye.

Abandoning my suitcase on the bed, I hurried to pry open the bedroom window and crawl outside. My heart pounded so loudly I was sure that they could hear it from inside the house. I went completely still, not trusting myself to shift for fear that my wolf would run back to him.

I stopped breathing entirely when I heard several people burst into my bedroom. It sounded like Jeremy and his beta, Neil, were talking with Ella, demanding to know where I was. Heavy steps searched my closet, and someone flipped my mattress on its side.

"She was in here recently. I can still smell her scent," a deep voice barked. It was the man from the hotel. *Our mate has arrived.*

I panicked and tried to calm my wolf's excitement as I tucked lower into the bush below my window. I could feel his presence above me, looking out the window, searching the air for my scent. He frowned and looked down. Our eyes met, and a slow smile crept over his god-like face. "Hello, little wolf."

Left with no other option, I shifted to my wolf form and instructed her to run as fast as she could. The direction didn't matter; all that mattered was putting as much distance between us as possible. She whined and protested at the sound of the male's angry roar from the window. She didn't have to look back for me to know that he, too, had shifted and was pursuing us.

My wolf's lungs and legs started to burn, not from the distance but from the strain of trying to move at full speed. She glanced back, and I pushed her to run faster after seeing how close the larger grey wolf was. He didn't even seem to be exerting himself in the chase. It was almost like he was playing with us, seeing how far my wolf would go before we surrendered.

From the corner of her eye, I saw another wolf leap from

a neighboring yard and tackle the grey wolf to the ground. *Patrick.*

My wolf panicked and turned to try and help him. His attack didn't harm the grey wolf at all, but his smaller black body would receive the brunt end of his opponent's frustration if she left. Preventing him from reaching his mate could earn Patrick the same fate as Alexander.

The grey wolf's eyes widened when she doubled back and stood between him and our best friend. Knowing that we were caught, I shifted to human form. My wolf's white and cream fur was quickly replaced with skin. Patrick shifted, too. He opened his arms to me, and I rushed to him. After a quick embrace, he held me back at arm's length, checking my body for any injuries.

The other wolf changed back, too, letting out an angry snarl as his bones snapped into place. I gasped at the sight of his naked body. His hair was down, falling long on his shoulders. He must have had it pulled up last night, but that wasn't what kept my attention. His tall frame was completely filled out with hard muscle, all except the appendage between his legs. Even flaccid, his dick was bigger than any I had seen before. Patrick bristled at my reaction, forcing me behind him so he could face the other man.

"Step away from my mate," the man growled, his wolf speaking through him. "I've already killed one fool for her honor, and I have no problem ending the life of another."

Patrick gave no indication that he heard the threat. Instead, he turned to look at me. His eyes urged me to run; he was willing to die slowing down the large grey wolf so that I could escape. But there was no way I would allow that to happen.

I walked around him, coming back into full view of the giant stranger. His gaze swept over me, causing his cock to harden and grow. I tore my eyes away from it, not wanting to see it get any larger.

"What do you want? I'll give you anything you want if you agree to leave in peace." My words caused an amused look to dance across his face.

"I like your fire. It will serve you well in our pack." His human eyes radiated with appreciation before traveling back to glare at Patrick. "However, no one should be seeing your naked form other than me. Especially not another man, such as the one hiding behind you."

Patrick's fangs elongated, and his eyes turned canine, but this time it wasn't from arousal or jealousy. I put my hand on his chest, trying to get him to relax.

The contact between us caused the stranger to shout his outrage again and rush to encircle my waist with his hand. He picked me up and planted me on his other side in a single, assertive motion.

"Little wolf, I will not have you touching other males." He hooked his hands under my legs and tossed me up over his shoulder. His long hair covered my ass, and my tits were pressed firmly against his back, shielding them from view.

Every inch of him felt hard and toned. I made fists with my hands and started pounding on his back, screaming at him to let me go.

"Patrick!" I called out to my friend in anguish. He stared helplessly, unsure of what to do. The shame of not being able to stop my kidnapping was evident in his features, causing me pain in a different way. I lost sight of him as the giant wolf deposited me in a shiny black car and locked the door.

I struggled with the latch, trying desperately to unlock it. He chuckled at my frantic movements as he slid into the driver's seat.

"Little wolf, you will find that your door cannot be unlocked from the inside. You'd do best to save your energy for the things I have planned for us."

He gave me a wicked look, and I shuddered. "I would never do anything with you. If you let me go, we can talk, but that's all I'm offering."

"We will talk, for it seems there is a lot we need to set straight between us," he agreed. "But make no mistake, you're mine, and I'm not letting you go."

His car pulled away from my house, leaving Ella alone in the front yard. I turned away from her, not wanting her to watch me become completely unglued.

I curled my knees in front of myself, doing my best to shield my breasts from his view. He did not comment on my lack of clothing or anything else until we were back at the Feldman Hotel.

After parking, he reached into the center console and tossed an XL T-shirt in my direction. As much as I wanted to disappear into the fabric, I made no attempt to put it on. I tilted my chin, challenging him to say something about it.

"We can sit here for as long as you like, but we are not leaving the car until you're covered." The stranger leaned back in his seat to get comfortable, letting me know that waiting for my cooperation was no issue for him.

"Why are you doing this to me?" I asked quietly, changing tactics, and hoping that he had a sensitive nature under the hard exterior. "I want to go home. Please take me home."

His eyes softened at my request. "I *will* take you home. My pack will be very excited to meet you."

It took every ounce of control I had not to rip the look of sympathy off his stupid face. I struggled to keep my expression innocent. "I want to go home with my family, not yours. Please just let me out of the car."

He stilled, searching my face. "I think," he said slowly. "That you are a very skilled actress. Growing up in a pack yourself, you must know that after we solidify our bond, your home will be with me."

"I don't want to mate with you. Or with anyone."

"What?" His voice hitched in surprise. Clearly, he was not expecting me to say that. To his credit, I was probably the only one of our kind who felt that way. "The goddess made us two halves of the same whole. We will mirror and complement each other perfectly. You're upset and not thinking rationally."

For a fleeting second, I felt horrible for the shadow of rejection that passed over him. But it was gone so quickly that I wasn't sure if I had imagined it.

"You knew I didn't want this. Why else would I run and hide from you?" I asked sharply.

He gave me a sheepish look. "I've heard of some females giving chase to make their mate prove his worth before agreeing to become his. I thought you were testing me. And, believe me, I would never back down from a challenge issued by you."

His eyes lit with renewed fire, and he took the opportunity to skim his gaze over my naked body. I gulped and pulled my knees back in front of myself, suddenly self-conscious. This was headed in the wrong direction. He frowned at my movement.

"Do not cover yourself with me. Your beauty was made for me and my eyes alone."

A new idea flickered in my mind, remembering his rage at the hotel. It was risky to set him off again, but maybe he would relent if he understood the extent of my sexual history.

"Others have seen me. Other men." I took a breath, trying to form the words correctly and not turn to goo under his heated stare. "Other men that I have had sex with. Plural. More than one."

The silence that followed was like someone had suctioned the air out of the car. I watched as he swallowed hard, like the information I had given him was painful to process. His hands shook slightly as he gripped the steering wheel, but when he finally spoke, his voice was even and eerily calm.

"I will need their names so I can hunt them down like the man in the hotel room. When I got there, and his sheets and body smelled of you, sealing his fate. These other men will be no different."

My heart sank as I realized that my words did not make him want me less. Instead, they just incited him to more violence. Without another word, I slid the shirt over my head and folded my arms, ready to leave the car.

He gave a short nod and left to come to the passenger's side and open my door. As soon as he crossed to the other side, I rushed to the driver's seat and forced his door open. The handle gave easily, and I spilled out onto the cement, shifting as I fell and landing on all fours.

At my direction, my wolf took off in a dead run across the parking lot, ignoring the reaction of our mate behind her. The fence around the hotel property was made of wood, and parts of it had broken away with age.

Her eyes searched for a break in the fencing large enough for her body, and she spotted a single missing panel. She was just small enough to make it out, but there was no way our pursuer would fit.

She slowed and forced her way through, wincing as the splintered wood caught on some of her fur and pierced her skin. Our mate was closing in, trying to force his way through the hole that was much too small for him. It held him for now, but it wouldn't be long until his strength allowed him to break one of the other panels. I called on her to turn and run. We needed every advantage we could get.

Chapter 4

At first, I wasn't sure where to send her. We couldn't go back home. That would be the first place he'd look. I groaned inwardly with frustration, remembering that my truck was still there. Our only way out of town was parked in my driveway, never mind the bag of clothes I packed. Or my cellphone. Or my wallet and money. The list went on and on.

We should go back to him and hear what he has to say. My wolf was eager to know more about the attractive male. I knew I was going to have difficulty convincing her to shift back with him on her mind, but being in human form would give us the best chance of escape. I could hide our scent with soap or cleaning solution as a human. I couldn't do the same as a wolf.

Maybe Patrick's house? The thought had its appeal. He had extra clothes for me, and he might even let me take his truck if I let him have mine.

My wolf ducked and turned toward the other side of town where Patrick lived, careful to avoid busy roads and houses. Jeremy and Neil might be out looking for her too, and I wasn't willing to risk running into one of them.

Keeping a steady pace allowed her to get to Patrick's place without taking any breaks. It also helped that the summer heat was winding down in favor of a cooler fall breeze.

Her ears flicked apprehensively as she approached the apartment complex, listening for anything that might be out of place. The male probably didn't know where Patrick lived, but that wouldn't prevent our alpha from stopping by.

Sure enough, Jeremy's voice alerted her of his presence before she could see him. My wolf ducked next to a trash can, and I prayed that the smell of old food was enough to mask her scent. He slammed Patrick's apartment door, grumbling to his beta as they walked to his truck.

"I know she's around here somewhere. She doesn't have a way out of town, and she knows Patrick would offer to help her leave," he grumbled darkly.

Neil shrugged. "If she leaves, wouldn't that bring balance back to the pack?"

Screw you, Neil. To him, I was just a problem to be solved. Thankfully, my alpha disagreed, and his chest rumbled with a warning to his second in command.

"She is a member of this pack, beta. It's my responsibility to not only maintain order but also ensure that she is happy and safe. Her true mate would provide both of those things for her. Just letting her wander out there alone is not an option."

Despite his foolishness, I felt my heart melt a little toward my alpha. He wasn't a cruel leader; he just wanted what was best for me in his own screwed-up way. Years of unbridled patriarchal thinking were probably to blame.

My wolf waited behind the trash cans longer than necessary, just to make sure that they were really gone. Slowly, she stood, and I begged her to shift. She tried once more to talk me into going back to the hotel, but I wouldn't budge. With an exaggerated sigh, she complied, and her fur disappeared once more.

Fully aware of my nudity, I crept to Patrick's back door and tapped lightly on the glass. He was there in an instant, eyes wide as he took in my body and settled his gaze back on my face. He slid the door open, guiding me into his kitchen.

"Are you okay? Goddess, Mare, I am so sorry I couldn't stop him from taking you. I figured if you got away, you'd probably come back here." He turned me around a few times, checking again for any injuries to my body.

I nudged him away softly. "He wouldn't hurt me...at least, I don't think he would. But I was lucky to get away. I'm not sure if I'd be able to give him the slip again."

I walked briskly back to his room and started pulling my clothes out of the drawers to take with me. He nodded curtly and went to the bathroom to gather more of my things. He returned with a gym bag and a mesh beach tote full of my shampoo, lotion, and makeup.

I pulled on one of my oversized sweaters and stepped into a pair of leggings, thankful to be covered again.

"They're coming back, you know," Patrick warned as he watched me dress. "They left to go search a few other places, but they'll be back in an hour or two."

I nodded, expecting as much. As exhausted as I was after the long run and as much as I wanted to curl up and kiss every inch of Patrick's body, I knew that there was no time.

"My keys and wallet are at home, along with my truck. Can I borrow yours?"

Patrick held up his keys and a roll of bills, tossing them to me one at a time. "I figured you'd need some help in that department."

He grabbed both bags and led me to the front door, pausing to look around before motioning for me to follow him. He placed the bags in the backseat and ducked inside the door to kiss me, both of us lingering longer than we should.

My nostrils flared when the scent hit me: my mate was close. He had either trailed me, or Jeremy told him where I might be. Patrick sensed him, too. He pulled back, slamming the door between us, and shouted at me to leave.

His truck was a much newer model than mine and it turned over easily. I shifted into gear, barreling out of the parking lot and onto the main road. I had to swerve at the last minute to miss the grey wolf who threw himself into my path. I had no desire to harm him, and if I did, I was sure my wolf would never forgive me.

I kept driving late into the night, only stopping once for gas and to use the restroom. Thanks to the gas station energy drink and the adrenaline coursing through my veins, my eyes stayed open and alert. Anytime a fancy black car crossed my path, I panicked, thinking it might be him.

Him. It was almost comical that I didn't know his name or anything about him. I had no idea what pack he was from or what he wanted with me besides probably someone to warm his bed.

We would know more if you hadn't forced us to run, my wolf complained.

I couldn't argue with that logic, but she assumed the very best about our mate and ignored all the major red flags. My thoughts drifted to Ella, hoping that she was alright and that she wasn't worried or upset with me. We might have our differences, but as much as I hated to admit it, I still wanted her approval.

After hours of using back roads and small highways, I felt confident that I had lost him. I pulled into an old motel after midnight, careful to park in the back between other cars. I even bothered to scrape the Dark Claw pack emblem bumper sticker off the back, praying that Patrick wouldn't mind when I returned the truck to him.

Of course, he won't mind, I chided myself. *He's your best friend. He cares more about your safety than a stupid sticker.*

Patrick and I had bonded over a lot of things over the years: we had similar temperaments and interests, neither of us held the same conservative beliefs as our pack, and more than anything, we wanted the other person to be safe and cared for.

If the goddess had any sense at all, she would have made us true mates based on those factors alone. Patrick had said as much many times, but I was always secretly glad that she didn't. I wasn't willing to give up my freedom for anyone, including Patrick.

When I finally reached the room, I made sure the locks on the door were secure and that the emergency fire window in the bathroom opened wide enough for me to squeeze out. It felt weird to be so on edge, but I knew that I'd have to get used to checking for alternate routes of escape. Being paranoid was my new normal.

I collapsed on the bed, using the TV for background noise

and a nightlight to help settle my nerves. When I finally did sleep, it was restless and full of nightmares. Maybe not nightmares, exactly, but there was a suffocating combination of panic and angry wolf snarls. It all sounded so close that I woke up in a cold sweat a few times, convinced that the grey wolf was there in my room. Each time I awoke, I was more relieved to find the room empty and quiet besides the chatter of the late-night home shopping network.

I gave up on sleep around eight in the morning, forcing myself from the lumpy mattress and into the shower. I used the shitty combination shampoo and conditioner to wash my hair and the small bar of motel soap to scrub my body. I wanted to save my own products in case I ran out of money and needed to camp in the car.

The miniature coffee pot provided a hot cup of caffeine, which also helped to perk me up. I sat on the bed, counting the money that Patrick had given me and trying to decide on my next course of action.

I had four hundred dollars; that was it. My heart sank because I knew it was probably all the money in Patrick's old coffee can. As a mechanic's apprentice, he made about the same amount as I did working at the library, but he had the added expense of having his own place. While the rent at the pack-owned apartment building was prorated, it was still more expensive than free. Hopefully, Ella would give him the money I had stashed in my bag. It wasn't four hundred dollars, but it was something.

I wiped a hand across my forehead. I had the room for another half hour before I needed to check out, and more importantly, I had to keep moving if I wanted to stay ahead of the grey wolf. I didn't know what kind of resources he had at his disposal, but if he was staying at the Feldman Hotel, it was probably more than mine.

I hesitated, debating whether I should call Ella or Patrick from the hotel phone. Those were the only numbers I knew by heart, and I wanted to let someone know that I wasn't dead. I picked up the receiver on the old phone and started to dial. Ella answered on the first ring.

"Mariam?" she asked, her voice anxious.

"Hi, Ella," I answered, twisting the cord through my fingers. "I just wanted to let you know that I'm okay. I won't be coming home for a long time, but I love you."

We weren't a family who talked about love very often and I could tell that my words threw her off a little bit. "Um…thanks. I love you too, Mare. Jeremy is really upset that you left, and Trace has taken off to find you, but I'm guessing you probably already know that…."

I frowned as she continued to ramble. Trace must be the name of the grey wolf.

"Listen, I need to go, but I'll talk to you again soon," I promised. She was about to protest, but I cut her off and hung up.

The clock on the wall said I still had fifteen minutes until I had to check out of the room and I really wanted to call Patrick, but Ella confirmed what I already knew: my mate was on my trail and I needed to leave as soon as possible.

I grabbed my things and hurried to Patrick's truck, tossing them both in the back. Tonight, I would have to sleep in the truck, maybe in the back under the stars. I needed the money for gas, and a motel bed wasn't much of an upgrade.

I drove in silence as if the radio might make too much noise and give away my location. Road signs told me when I entered one state and left another, but they revealed little else.

I had started out in Northern California, but I had already driven through Nevada and entered Utah a few hours earlier. I was bolder now, using the main interstates instead of sticking to the more rural roads. Since I only had a free map from a gas station to guide me, I couldn't really afford to get lost in some backwoods town. With no phone, I had no GPS.

I sucked in a sharp breath, remembering that Jeremy had tracking information placed on all pack member's phones, just in case there was an emergency, or someone went missing. The fact that I had to leave my phone behind was actually a blessing in disguise.

Night rolled in again, and I found a Walmart parking lot to settle into. It wasn't an ideal place to camp because I had to sleep on the bench seat in the back instead of shifting and sleeping in the bed, but the lighted area made me feel safe, and at least there was a bathroom where I could freshen up in the morning.

I killed the engine and crawled into the back. I used a rolled-up sweater as a pillow, vowing that tomorrow morning I would splurge and buy a blanket from the big box store.

I slept restlessly again. This time there was a lot of men shouting. Or maybe I was the one shouting in a man's voice. It was hard to tell what was going on exactly, but the whole thing was exhausting. I woke up a sweaty mess, desperate to get outside and feel the fresh air.

I eased out of the back, grabbing my toothbrush and toothpaste from my pack, and shoving them in the pocket of my sweater. Walmart might be forgiving, but I didn't want to advertise that I was using them as a makeshift B&B.

One clean mouth and a new flannel blanket later, I was back in the cab drumming my fingers on the steering wheel. I had escaped, and I was surviving, but for how long? I needed to find a job and a place to stay if I wanted to last for any real stretch of time away from my pack.

My wolf also needed other shifters to commune with, but I was worried about what other packs might already know about me and my situation. There were rare stories of wolves being returned to their alpha if they tried to leave and join a new pack. Whether that was a mandatory obligation or just a courtesy was a mystery to me.

I cursed myself for not knowing more about werewolf laws and politics. I worked in the pack's library, for crying out loud. All that information had been right there, at my fingertips. A human library wouldn't have the answers. Most of them were entirely unaware of our existence. And any information posted online wouldn't necessarily be reliable. I groaned in frustration.

Maybe, if I could find a pack and stay just long enough to use their library, I could get some answers. I could make up a story about just passing through if anyone questioned why I was there. I could even provide a fake name.

Happy to have a plan, I needed to decide which pack I should visit. It had to be one that was not directly aligned with Dark Claw, and they had to be friendly enough not to close off their borders to visitors. One pack stood out in my mind: Tumblewild. The Tumblewild pack was known for being more progressive in some ways, and I knew they were open to visitors, and possibly even new members.

I was raised to believe that the only reason to visit another pack was to search for your true mate, and that only applied to males. For females, the only reason to leave your pack was if your true mate belonged to a different one.

It was refreshing when I learned that some other wolves didn't share those feelings. In my mind, if someone wasn't happy with where they were living, they should be allowed to leave.

Fortunately, Tumblewild wasn't all that far away. It was located just north of Flagstaff, Arizona. A quick look at the map, and I was able to get back on the interstate, this time heading south.

Chapter 5

I drove through the night, not wanting to stop and sleep in the desert. The wide-open expanse might be a good choice for my wolf, but it also felt like there was nowhere for me to hide. Besides, it seemed like my dreams were getting worse and more realistic each night, which made me willing to skip having them altogether. I had other things to worry about, anyway.

Like Patrick's huge-ass truck, for example. It might be reliable, but it got horrible gas mileage. I was in no position to complain about it since beggars couldn't be choosers, but aside from buying a few gas station coffees and a drive-thru burger, I was saving all my money and praying that I wouldn't run out of gas. If gas prices stayed about the same in Arizona, I would only have about fifty bucks left when I rolled into town. If they didn't…well, I didn't want to think about that.

Despite my dwindling funds, I was very thankful for the Walmart blanket I bought. I wrapped it around me in the driver's seat, imagining that the warmth was another wolf to snuggle with.

I reached the Tumblewild pack just as the sun was coming up. The sight of the houses clustered together around an impressive downtown gave me the boost of energy that I needed. Some kids were playing outside in the early morning sun, letting me know that there was no school today. *What day was it even? Saturday? Sunday?*

I parked the truck next to the town hall building and got out to stretch my legs. The hall would probably be where the alpha held pack meetings. Smaller packs might use a school or library for such things, but it looked like Tumblewild was fairly well-off.

There was a row of shops on one side of the street, and the other side housed a school, post office, diner, and library. I grinned broadly when I spotted the library on the end; I had always loved to read and getting to spend my time around books had been the best job ever. And now, it might be the only place where I could find answers about any options I had to avoid mating with Trace.

I walked straight there, praying that it wasn't locked. I let out a sigh of relief when the door handle turned for me.

"Good morning." The librarian behind the circulation desk greeted me with a cheery smile. She gave me a curious look, probably trying to guess who I was and what I was doing in Tumblewild.

"Good morning," I said in return. "I am looking for a few different items. Do you mind if I browse the shelves?"

I wanted to go directly to where werewolf law collections were kept but decided against it. That would be a huge red flag. In the four years I worked at the library, the only people who looked through those old books were council members. It definitely wasn't typical for some random wolf passing through to ask about them.

She nodded, returning her attention to some of the periodicals she was sorting. I walked away, trying to look casual as I wandered over to the fiction section. If I stayed and looked at a regular book or two, it might be less suspicious when I drifted over to the pack bylaw area.

Several minutes passed as I pretended to be interested in a random historical romance novel. The librarian at the circulation desk seemed genuinely busy, which emboldened me to inch closer to the heavy wooden door that separated the public library from the space specifically for pack members. It wasn't labeled, but I recognized it instantly for what it was. When she stopped to help another patron, I seized the opportunity to slip inside.

The room was filled from floor to ceiling with dark burgundy hardcover books. Shelves and tables broke up the space and created a maze, making it impossible to see how big the area truly was from the entrance.

I could hear the turning of a page from somewhere in the back and caught the scent of a male werewolf, alerting me to the fact that I wasn't alone. With any luck, he would stay hidden while I looked for what I needed to find.

I ran my fingers across the collection kept next to the door. I loved the way the glossy leather binding felt under my fingertips. The ornate gold writing on the spines indicated the year of the volume and whether it contained specific Tumblewild pack code or broader werewolf law.

Keeping this section tucked away helped prevent the occasional human visitor from stumbling upon it. The pack's library was just an average small-town public building to someone unaware of werewolves living among humans.

I quickly scanned the new-looking volumes and paused at the one labeled with last year's date. It looked insanely heavy, and as I pulled it from the shelf, I confirmed that it was just as weighty as it appeared.

"Need some help?" The male wolf voice didn't wait for an answer as he reached past me to grab the book with a single hand. I suppressed the desire to roll my eyes at the ease with which he held it. *Show off.*

When I turned, his easy smile erased the sarcastic response I was going to give him. He looked young. While he was probably about my age, or maybe even a little older, his clean-shaven face and slim build took years off his appearance.

"Thanks," I said as he set it on the counter-height table in the center of the room. Since these books couldn't be checked out, the table was necessary for members of the pack to study them.

He nodded, looking at me with interest. "I haven't seen you in Tumblewild before. Are you stopping through on vacation or something?"

The way he phrased it felt like he was trying to help me come up with a reason for being there, almost like he already knew a real one didn't exist. "Something like that. I just wanted to look up some of the formal laws while I was here, to know when I would be wearing out my welcome."

I had rehearsed the explanation during the long drive. It felt plausible enough that another pack might buy it. The male werewolf raised a single eyebrow but nodded his understanding. He retreated to return to where he was studying one of the older manuscripts. It wasn't even a bound copy, instead just a rolled-up scroll.

My mouth dropped open when I saw it. The Dark Claw library had some old copies of werewolf law but nothing that was written on a scroll. I abandoned the new document and followed the male wolf to see it up close.

I smiled as I leaned closer to the ancient page, hovering, and not daring to touch it with my bare hands. The words were written in an old werewolf language, one that I recognized belonging to wolves in the southwest, although it wasn't anything I could read myself.

"You like old stuff or something?" I jumped a little at the question. I was so distracted by the scroll that I had forgotten he was still in the room.

"Yeah, I guess I do. I love all old books but scrolls like this are so rare." I stepped away from his workspace reluctantly. "It's beautiful."

"It really is, isn't it?" His eyes flickered to my neck, checking for a mating bite. When he didn't find one, he stuck out his hand. "I'm Gabe, by the way. And you are?"

"Ella. Ella Landis," I answered, thankful that my sister's name was common enough not to raise alarm. If any werewolves were searching for Mariam Hinder, they wouldn't think to look twice at Ella Landis. I had always preferred my mother's maiden last name, anyway, and it felt good to make use of it.

"Thanks for your help, Gabe. Enjoy the scroll." I left the male werewolf and walked back to my table and barstool. Hours passed as I poured over the text. My stomach growled angrily from being neglected for so long. It had been over a day and a half since I had eaten the fast-food cheeseburger.

"It sounds like you could use a break," Gabe said, joining me at the table again. I blushed, knowing that he heard my growling stomach. There wasn't much that could get past werewolf hearing, especially in a small, quiet place like this.

"You're probably right. Do you know when the library closes?" I still needed to check a few things, but it felt like I was getting closer to finding some answers.

"Today, it closes at six. We have a pack run tonight, so everything is going to shut down around then."

I nodded, hating that my wolf wouldn't be able to join the others on the run. We weren't members of the pack, so we wouldn't be welcome to take part. Maybe I could take us to the outskirts of town and give her a chance to run on her own out there.

"Let's go," Gabe held out a hand to help me off the stool. I accepted it and followed him out, glancing at the clock on the wall as we left. It was already one-thirty and well past time for breakfast. If I bought lunch, maybe my wolf would be able to catch a rabbit or something to avoid paying for dinner. She nodded, excited at the opportunity to hunt.

Gabe led me to the diner I saw earlier on Main Street. It was busy, but we found an empty booth in the back. I studied him as he looked at the one-page paper menu.

He reminded me of Patrick in some ways, even though he was much slimmer. My heart clenched at the thought, hoping that my friend was alright back home and that our alpha wasn't blaming him for my escape.

"So, what's good here?" I asked, eager for a distraction from my thoughts.

"My favorite is the meatloaf, but the menu changes every day. Today, the two entree options are beef stew or a club sandwich. They're probably going light because there will be a lot of food at the bonfire tonight."

I had to smile at the way my wolf grinned at the mention of a bonfire. Dark Claw usually had one after a pack run if it wasn't raining, too. Nothing worked up an appetite more than running with other wolves.

"I think I'll have the beef stew. It's been a while since I've had something like that."

Gabe nodded. "That's the better choice, to be honest. Maggie does a good job with most things, but the club sandwiches are kind of dry."

"You're dead meat when I tell her you said that, Gabe," A pretty waitress appeared next to our booth and set down water glasses in front of us. Her eyes smiled at the joke and the way Gabe turned pale from her threat.

"You wouldn't dare. This is the only restaurant within walking distance of town hall. A single guy like me would starve."

"If the single part is a problem, I've already offered to fix that for you," the girl answered, eyebrows raised.

I choked on my water, not fully believing what I was hearing. Flirting hardly ever happened between unmated wolves at Dark Claw, and when it did, females were never the instigators. She quirked an eyebrow at my reaction, assessing me more closely now.

"Do I have some new competition here, Gabriel?"

Gabe gave me an apologetic glance and scowled at the waitress. "Cool it, Samantha. She's just new in town and needed something to eat. Besides, we've been over this before; we're just friends."

"For now," she said, rolling her eyes. "Okay, *friend*, what do you want?"

"We'll both have the stew," Gabe answered, trying his best to look annoyed but failing at it. Their relationship was odd at best, but they seemed to like each other, so I remained quiet and sipped my water until the waitress left.

"Sorry about Samantha. She's probably my best friend, but she can come on a little strong, especially if you aren't used to her." Gabe unwrapped his straw and took a long drink from his glass. "So, where are you from, Ella?"

"The east coast," I lied. My mother's pack was from Massachusetts, so it only made sense to say I was a member of her pack if I was going to use her last name. "I just wanted to travel a bit and see some other packs along the way."

Gabe nodded slowly, considering my words. If he didn't believe me, he made no comment about it. Samantha returning with rolls and two bowls of hot soup that saved me from having to manufacture any more lies.

The beef stew warmed me from the inside out, and my wolf was thankful for the nourishment. If we were going to shift tonight, she would need the strength that the hearty meal provided. I reached for the check when it came, but Gabe snatched it up first.

"Don't worry about it. It's not every day that a mysterious and beautiful new wolf comes to town," he said, eyes twinkling with humor.

I blushed and mumbled a thank you before following him out. My first date had been with Alexander, which could mean that this was my second date since he was picking up the tab. My wolf snarled at the idea of starting a romantic relationship with the new male. She had her heart set on getting to know our mate better, and she wasn't interested in Gabe in the slightest.

I had to agree with her, at least about not pursuing anything with our new acquaintance. My full stomach clenched with guilt remembering how the date with Alexander had ended. Nope. No one else was going to die if, for some reason, Trace was able to track me down in Tumblewild.

"So, what all are you looking for in here? At the risk of sounding really boring, I spend a lot of time in the Pack Collections room. Maybe I can help you," Gabe offered when we were back inside the library.

I chewed on the inside of my cheek. His expertise might be helpful. I kept hitting dead-ends, and the library would be closing in an hour. Maybe I could explain enough to get his help without having to say it all.

"My alpha wants me to mate with a certain wolf and I'm not interested. I was wondering if there was any way I could get out of it when I return home."

I was careful to leave out the part about being true mates; I already knew there was nothing I could do about that. Even alphas couldn't stand between a couple that the goddess had brought together. It would take one of us bonding with another wolf to break that connection.

Gabe gave me a look of compassion. "Your alpha doesn't sound very smart if he is trying to force couplings. He must not care that some wolves wish to find their true mates instead of settling for just playing house."

I blinked at his judgmental statement. Lots of wolves in Dark Claw wanted to wait for their true mates, but those who mated with others weren't considered second-class citizens. They might be lonely, or their true mate might have died. Some get tired of waiting and want pups before they get too old.

The look on my face must have betrayed my feelings, and Gabe groaned apologetically. "That came out wrong. There's nothing wrong with regular, chosen matings, but most alphas agree that forcing them is unethical."

I nodded my agreement at his clarification, wanting to just move past the awkward moment. In my mind, all werewolf matings were unethical because it gave the male the upper hand over the female. The male's rules were law for her unless their alpha stepped in to negate them, and if she were unfortunate enough to be mated to the alpha, then she was just shit out of luck. But the optimistic werewolf standing in front of me probably felt differently about mating since he would be the one giving the orders and not receiving them.

Gabe flipped through some of the pages in the large book, scanning the headings before stopping abruptly.

"Here," he said, pointing to a paragraph at the bottom of the page. "It says that alphas may not require members of their pack to mate with anyone other than their true mate unless a quorum of ten pack alphas supports the decree."

So, Ella had been wrong about Jeremy being able to mate me to any random wolf in the pack on a whim. She probably said that just to scare me, which was irritating, but the new information gave me an idea. Maybe I could convince Jeremy that Trace wasn't my true mate. My wolf flicked her ears, annoyed at the thought of lying to our alpha or trying to escape our fate with Trace. Sometimes we were so different that I wondered how we were technically the same animal.

The librarian from the front desk cracked the door open and reminded us that the library would be closing soon. I tried to play it cool, nodding along with Gabe at her words, like I belonged there just as much as he did.

Armed with this new information, I stepped aside so Gabe could shelve the enormous book. We left the library together, both deep in thought. I was curious about what Gabe was mulling over but figured it would be too intrusive to ask.

He walked me to my car and frowned. "Where are you staying while you're here?"

I felt like he had already guessed the truth, but I found myself embarrassed anyway. "I'm just going to camp out under the stars. My wolf will enjoy it."

"Camping can be fun, but not when it's the only option," he answered slowly, studying my face. "I have a spare room at my place. Why don't you hang out there tonight while the pack goes on a run? You said yourself that you weren't going to be here forever, so there's no point in looking for your own place."

My cheeks reddened even more at his offer. *Does he think that we want to sleep with him?* I asked my wolf, hoping she was intuitive enough to see his real motives. She rolled her eyes and huffed before curling up to sleep. Clearly, she didn't view him as a threat to our safety, but he seemed to sense the reason behind my reluctance.

"It wouldn't be anything more than just roommates," he blurted. "I'm waiting for my true mate…in case you were worried about…you know…."

I smiled at the way he trailed off without finishing his sentence. "Thanks," I said, offering him a genuine smile.

"I'd like that. I promised my wolf that we would go running tonight, too. Can I meet you after the pack run?"

"Sure," he said with a grin. He scribbled down his address on my map and gave me some quick directions from the library. He seemed concerned that I didn't have a cell phone or any method of GPS, but he let it go and wished me well on my run.

Back in the car, I ducked my head and said a quick prayer of thanks to the goddess. In all likelihood, she wasn't interested in my prayers since I had no intention of following the mating rules she established for my kind at the beginning of our creation, but I wanted to offer what I could to her anyway.

I tried to push aside my outrage about having a true mate and needing to leave my friends. I didn't want to complain to her again about how females had to defer to their mates. I wanted to just be grateful for the blessings I had received that day, namely a full belly and a place to stay that wasn't outdoors. Who knows, maybe I would even find more happiness in Tumblewild than I did back home.

My wolf howled with pleasure as she raced through the woods. The outskirts of Flagstaff offered acres of unfenced terrain that gave her exactly what she needed: space to run. She flexed her paws, savoring the feel of the fertile earth beneath them. She ran until her chest heaved, and then she fell on her back and rolled on the cool grass like a goofball. If I wouldn't allow her to be with the grey wolf, this was the next best thing, and I was happy to provide it for her.

In the distance, we could hear the howls of the

Tumblewild pack as they enjoyed their run together. My wolf whined and howled again, wanting desperately to join them. Her thoughts raced back to memories of running with our pack. Ella's and my wolf always had a much stronger relationship than I did with my sister, probably because they didn't butt heads the way we did as humans.

I offered her memories of my own from our runs with Patrick and others from Lance chasing us through the woods near the schoolhouse during recess when we were kids. She rumbled, agreeing that those were good memories, too.

We stayed out as late as we could, with her weaving through the trees and howling with the pack in the distance. Finally, she gave me back control, and I slipped into my clothes. I was spent but felt rejuvenated and full of life for the first time since I left home. I turned over the engine and drove to Gabe's, trying hard not to get lost in the process.

Chapter 6

I left my bed late in the morning, this time without the panic I experienced in the motel, but still inexplicably tired from a night of tossing and turning. My dreams had gotten so violent and angry that they should probably be classified as nightmares. They were confusing, too, because it was like I was surrounded by a thick fog that muffled everything going on around me.

Gabe's apartment was close to the library, which was a relief because I knew I needed to start looking for work. Given my experience, a job there was probably the only thing I was qualified to do.

"Good morning, sleepyhead," Gabe greeted me and whistled at my change in appearance. He gestured to the coffee pot, inviting me to get some for myself.

"Good morning. Thanks again for letting me stay with you, Gabe," I said. I filled a mug and leaned against the counter. Showering with my own shampoo, putting on a little makeup, and wearing clothes that actually fit made me feel more like myself again. "Do you know if anyone in town is hiring?"

Gabe's eyebrows shot up in surprise. "I didn't think you would be staying long enough to want to look for work." His response was slow, as though he was trying not to say the wrong thing and offend me.

That caused me to hesitate, too. "I'm not planning on staying forever, but my traveling has gotten more expensive than I thought, and I need to make some money before I leave."

There was something he wasn't telling me. I waited, hoping he would spill it without me having to ask. It felt wrong to pressure my host to divulge information, especially when he was allowing me to crash at his place for free. When he refused to break the silence, I did with a sigh.

"Is there something that I need to know about spending time in Tumblewild?" I asked.

"Actually, I wasn't sure how to bring this up, but wolves from other packs aren't allowed to live in Tumblewild indefinitely. Our borders are open to visitors, but anyone staying more than three months has to receive approval from our alpha." Gabe's Adam's apple bobbed, and he looked a little uncomfortable. "Our alpha has only approved new members a few times. Other than when a pack member takes on a mate from another pack, of course. So, I am not sure how successful your petition would be."

So much for being a progressive pack, I thought. I forced a smile, trying to relieve his discomfort. "Three months is plenty of time. I'll be gone long before your alpha feels the need to throw me out."

I meant the comment to be lighthearted, but it caused Gabe to furrow his brow. *He doesn't agree with the rule,* my wolf said. It was true; the idea of turning wolves away from

Tumblewild seemed to really bother him. I reached out to touch his arm, hoping he understood that I wasn't upset about the policy. If I could start working right away, I would be able to save more than enough to get me to another pack. Or maybe by then, I could even return home.

Gabe cleared his throat and took a step back, causing my hand to drop to my side. "I think that the pack's school is hiring. What with the teacher shortage and all, you know?"

It was my turn to look concerned. "I've never taught before, and I'm definitely not licensed to teach in Arizona. Thanks for the suggestion, though."

He shook his head. "I think they're hiring teacher's assistants, too. No experience required. It might be worth a look anyway. I can't think of anyone else looking for short-term employees, but it wouldn't hurt to ask around. In any case, I have to get to work, too."

"What do you do for the pack?" I asked, happy for a change of topic.

"I'm a council apprentice. One day, I'll sit on the pack's council, but for today, I'm just going to read some old documents and get coffee and make phone calls for my mentor while he is out of town."

"So, you were working yesterday?"

He nodded, grabbing his suit jacket off the back of a kitchen chair. "A little unpaid overtime, you know?" He put his mug in the sink and riffled through one of the draws until he found a spare key. He handed it to me, causing my eyes to widen with surprise. "I've got a good feeling about you, Ella. Good luck on the job search today. I'll see you tonight around six."

And with that, he walked out the door and left me, a total

stranger, alone in his apartment. I stood, rubbing the key between my fingers. While my wolf didn't understand the significance of the key, she shared in my confusion about him.

Guilt settled in the pit of my stomach when I thought about him calling me Ella. Gabe trusted me enough to offer a key to his place, and I didn't even trust him enough to tell him my real name. I pushed the feeling to the side, knowing there was nothing that I could do to change it.

I waited nervously in the school's office, knowing the chances of me being hired were little to none. I didn't have a driver's license, a resume, or even professional references. I might be able to provide Patrick as a personal reference, but it's not like he was a former coworker. If I listed the librarian at my old job, she would go straight to Jeremy with information about where I was hiding out. No, asking her to put in a good word for me wasn't an option.

"Ms. Landis?" The principal appeared in the doorway of her office. She smiled and motioned for me to follow her. I let out a slow breath, thankful to at least be wearing a more professional outfit than sweats and a T-shirt.

"Have a seat," she said, gesturing to the set of chairs in front of her desk. "I must say, Ms. Landis, that you come to us highly recommended. When can you start?"

I lowered myself into the chair, not believing what she said. "Um…I'm sorry, Ms. Jenner. I come recommended by whom?"

"By Mr. Daniels, of course." The confusion must have been written across my face, causing her to laugh. "Gabe.

Gabriel Daniels. In this pack, if Gabe recommends you, you're hired. He's an excellent judge of character, and, well, I think he has done more favors for everyone in Tumblewild than we'd like to admit. So, when can you start?"

"I don't have any documentation. I left my last pack… in a hurry. Don't you need background checks and driver's licenses and stuff to work in a school?"

"We are a pack school, Ms. Landis. Our hiring practices don't need to conform with the norms of the human world, especially since almost all our employees are hired from within the pack. In your case, Mr. Daniels' recommendation is more than enough."

"I can start immediately," I said, choking the words out. "I can only stay on temporarily, though. As a non-pack member, I have to leave before my three months are up."

Ms. Jenner nodded. "Yes, Gabe mentioned that when he called. Right now, I am more than willing to take all the help I can get. Two of our teachers have taken a leave of absence, so you will assist both kindergarten classes. Is that something you can handle?"

"Absolutely. I love kids." I smiled at the thought of a room full of young pups.

"Wonderful! The dress code is casual since we run after little ones all day. Heather at the front desk will help you with the paperwork, and you can start tomorrow. The hours are seven-thirty to four, Monday through Friday."

I was grinning from ear to ear as I walked into the Tumblewild town hall building. In one hand, I held a cup of fresh coffee and in the other a to-go box filled with a generous helping of meatloaf from the diner we visited the night before. I stopped at the front desk, unsure where to find Gabe or even if I would be allowed to personally give him the meal.

"Good afternoon, I am here to deliver lunch for Gabriel Daniels," I said when the receptionist turned toward me. "Should I leave it here, or can I go to his office?"

The female wolf didn't try to hide her excitement. "You must be Ella. I'm Linda. It's so good to meet you." She leaned over the counter and extended her hand. I set the coffee down to shake it, grateful to find another friendly face. "Gabe mentioned that he had a friend from out of town staying with him."

"It's good to meet you, too," I said. I tried not to show any surprise at the way Gabe had explained our friendship. It was kind of him to act like we were old friends rather than what we actually were: strangers who had just met each other less than a day ago.

She smiled at my shy response and used the phone at her desk to call Gabe downstairs. Her eyes twinkled when she mentioned that a special friend was waiting for him.

Gabe must have guessed who the special friend was. His smile grew to match my own when I handed him the coffee and meatloaf. He turned to go back to his office, motioning for me to follow him into the elevator.

"Thank you so much for the recommendation, Gabe. Ms. Jenner hired me on the spot!"

It took everything I had in me to wait until he was seated at his desk to share the good news. He gave me a knowing look and struggled to keep a straight face.

"I bet. You don't look like you've done any hard time and

they are desperate for help," he said.

I wanted to reach across the table and nudge him for the dismissive comment, but I resisted, remembering how he had pulled away from me that morning. While I certainly wasn't trying to flirt with him, Gabe seemed concerned about any touching at all, and I wanted to respect his boundaries. So, I rolled my eyes instead.

"Yeah, I'm sure that was it."

"So, when do you start, Ella?" he asked, taking his first bite of meatloaf.

I had to grit my teeth together not to correct him with my real name. "Tomorrow, seven-thirty in the morning. So, I might have to be the one setting the coffee pot."

He laughed again, adding some of the mashed potatoes to his fork. "You slept in today, but tomorrow you'll see that I was already up for a few hours before you even came out of your room. Unless you plan on waking up at five, I'll continue making the coffee."

I should have known that he was an early riser. He probably had a whole morning routine.

"So, what do people do for fun in Tumblewild? I'm assuming there's not another pack run this evening."

He shook his head. "No such luck. We only have them about once a month during the full moon unless our alpha calls for an additional one."

"I haven't met your alpha. Do I need to introduce myself to him?" I wrung my hands under the desk, suddenly worried and hoping that I hadn't offended the leader of the pack by not seeking him out already.

Jeremy expected visitors to introduce themselves as soon as possible, and he was the only alpha I knew. His expectation made sense; the alpha was charged with the pack's safety, and to protect the pack, he had to keep tabs on everyone who entered.

To my relief, Gabe shook his head. "I texted our beta after you settled in last night. Visitors usually go through him, since Tumblewild is pretty large and our alpha stays busy with other things. Lately, he's been even more swamped than usual. He wasn't even at the pack run."

I shot him a surprised look. Jeremy never missed a pack run. He said it was an important time for him to connect with everyone and it was one of the reasons the pack looked forward to them so much.

Gabe shrugged and shook his head, agreeing with me without saying as much.

"So, was your beta alright with me staying here until my visitor's pass expires?"

Gabe's ears turned pink, which must have been his own version of blushing. "He welcomed you to stay at Tumblewild. He was…skeptical…of you staying with me, but that's only because he knows that I want to pursue my true mate. I plan on touring some packs next summer to see if I can find her."

I tried and failed to stifle a laugh. His beta was afraid that Gabe was going to bone me. "You know that wolves can have sex without claiming each other, right? Does he know that?"

"Of course. But it is the belief of my pack that the goddess requires her wolves to be celibate until mating, and I want to uphold that law for myself. Besides, something tells me that it will be worth it when I find her." His explanation was simple, and he made no apology for it.

"I think that's very romantic, Gabe. For what it's worth, I promise that I am not secretly after your virginity." His ears deepened to a darker shade of red, but that was the only indication of his discomfort. The rest of him relaxed like he had been a little worried about ulterior motives on my end.

"I should get out of your hair. I know that you still have a lot to get done, but I just wanted to say thanks for everything. I mean it, Gabe. I didn't know what I was going to do when I got here."

Gabe stood with me, coming around the desk to show me out. "You're very welcome, Ella. I kind of had that impression when we met, and like I said, I just had a good feeling about you."

Outside, the sun was high in the sky, and a slight breeze was in the air. My wolf lifted her nose, content with the feeling of the wind in my hair. If I hadn't taken her for a run the day before, she would have been begging to shift. As it was, she circled a few times and promptly fell asleep.

Despite sleeping well after Gabe, I was eager to join her. Maybe I would finally get some rest without having any crazy nightmares.

I went back to Gabe's, ensuring that the door was locked behind me. I changed and slipped beneath the sheets. It took me no time at all to settle on the comfortable mattress and fall asleep.

At first, it seemed like I would get my wish, but soon my mind was taken over with deep male voices. Their words were fuzzy and unintelligible, almost like I was hearing them underwater. Slowly, they started to get clearer.

"I don't care where you've looked. You aren't searching hard enough." The shiver that I felt run down my spine told me immediately that the voice belonged to my mate.

The wolves he spoke to must be fools. They should be terrified, but all they did was laugh and shake their heads. One, the largest in the group, answered him.

"The guys are doing the best they can, Trace. We've got every tracker there is searching nearby packs and roadside hotels. I've got to hand it to your girl; she's a sly one." The man leaned over a pool table, angling his stick to take a shot. I felt my mate's frustration at the way he was being dismissed.

"You know," another wolf added. "You'd probably get farther with her if you tried to charm her a little more, and huffed and puffed a little less. She might not be running out of rebellion. She might just be scared of you. Have you thought of that?"

Trace grumbled a response, and the feeling of his disbelief was strong. *She knows I'd never hurt her. She's my true mate. I want to cherish her, worship her...discipline her...*

Explicit images of us flashed through his mind, causing him to become horny and me to panic. I clawed at the darkness to try and wake myself up. My stirring drew his attention, and I felt his confusion replace his arousal. *Little wolf, is that you?*

I refused to answer and tried to calm myself. How was I able to hear him? Or see through his eyes? He hadn't bitten me. We hadn't even kissed, much less had sex. Those things were required for a clear and strong bond. And yet, the goddess was nonetheless allowing me access to his mind and emotions.

Even worse, this connection wasn't one-way. He could sense my emotions, too. I felt his excitement and joy burst through my body. I felt his wave of positive emotions ebb and flow, incorporating others like disappointment and confusion over me running away. And there, just beneath the surface, was the deeply rooted jealousy that he harbored against any man I had contact with. He moved for the door without offering any explanation to the others in the room.

I heard them voice concern and ask where he was going, but I knew. He wanted to be alone to focus on us. I could see a hallway and a beautifully decorated office before he finally stopped in an ornate bedroom. He locked the door behind him and settled onto the bed.

Mariam, please talk to me.

His voice rolled over me, calming the anxiety I felt initially about the connection. I formed the words in my mind, testing his ability to hear me. *What do you want with me, grey wolf?*

I felt his wolf join in his joy, yipping and acting like a puppy, happy to be acknowledged. My wolf came forward, eager to see him, too.

Our wolves know each other, mate. We are fated. Written in the stars. That's the only way this discussion is possible.

The way he talked tempted me to listen to what he was saying. His voice was almost hypnotic. Refusing to be swayed, I forced myself to remain grounded in reality.

Even if that's true, I do not want to be mated. I want my freedom.

Trace growled low. *I spoke to your former alpha. He informed me of the type of freedom you have been enjoying.*

It's not just about sex, I countered. *I want to be able to do what I want and have the friends I want, too. Being mated to a male werewolf would be suffocating, and I have a feeling you would be worse than most.*

He grunted, not denying his controlling nature. *This is the way of our kind, little wolf. You'll see. I love rewarding obedience.*

Again, images of us together assaulted my mind. I wanted to look away, but there was nowhere to avert my gaze. I drank in the scene of him pounding into me, hand wrapped around my hair to keep me securely in place. In his vision, I screamed and begged him for more.

Two could play that game. I concentrated on an image of my own, showing him my night with Alexander. The large man had lowered his head to feast on my core. My legs were hoisted high over his shoulders as he brought me to orgasm again and again.

The fury radiating off Trace startled me out of the dream and propelled me back into consciousness.

Chapter 7

Trace threw the closest thing to him -an alarm clock, shattering it and leaving an indent in the drywall. Any misgivings he had about killing his mate's lover were gone. In fact, he was disappointed that he had been so merciful about the idiot's death. Trace had snapped the shifter's neck as soon as he caught Mariam's scent in the hotel room, just as his wolf demanded. He should have made him suffer and beg for forgiveness before ending his life.

The rational side of Trace's brain told him that he should also be angry with Mariam. She broke the laws of celibacy. She should have been waiting for *him*. For *them*.

"Are you alright, Trace?" His beta Randy's voice was faint on the other side of the thick door. He raked his hands through his hair as he got up and unlocked it for the beta. They were like brothers, and Trace could use his support now more than ever.

"She doesn't want me. Mariam rejected me." His voice shook, this time with a more vulnerable emotion.

Randy looked around the room, confused. "Is she here?"

"No, she isn't," Trace answered, pouring them each a

glass of scotch. He offered one to Randy, and it was accepted without a word. "I could hear her in my head. I could see what she saw, and she could do the same with me."

The beta let out a low whistle. "That seems odd, given that you two haven't… you know…."

Trace glared at him. His inability to mate and claim Mariam was a sore spot, now more than ever. "No, we haven't. But apparently, that hasn't stopped her from fucking every damn wolf in the Dark Claw pack."

Randy's eyes widened. He was with Trace when Jeremy had provided some background information on Mariam. He had mentioned that she'd become close with some of the other young male wolves. That's the way he put it… she had become *close* with them. Both Randy and Trace knew what that had meant, and it had taken every ounce of restraint for them not to attack her former alpha for implying such things about her.

But if the image she sent to Trace was an actual memory, Jeremy's word choice had been as tactful as possible.

"Do you want to reconsider pursuing her? You are well within your right to choose a different mate."

Randy didn't need to tell him that. Trace knew werewolf law backward and forward. But this was the she-wolf that the goddess had created for him, no matter what was in her past. He had to reach her, convince her to accept our bond, and then she would become his perfect mate.

"No," he said, his resolve more potent than ever. "Mariam is mine, the only one worthy of standing by my side. I just need to find her and remind her of her place."

Trace threw back the last of the alcohol, enjoying the smooth flavor of the expensive drink. "The first thing I ever promised her was that I would meet any challenge she gave me, and I will not fail her now with weakness." Randy grinned his approval and slapped his alpha on the back. He would help Trace find her and ensure he kept my word.

After taking a few moments to compose himself, Trace returned to discuss the next course of action with the rest of his men. He felt a twinge of guilt when he entered the room and saw them all sitting there, waiting for their new orders.

He had reassigned the entire leadership team, requiring them to forgo their typical pack duties to help search for Mariam, but none of them seemed to mind the change. They were all very invested in recovering the she-wolf who would help their alpha lead our pack.

Despite their willingness to help, the younger, unmated men had been particularly alarmed by Trace's recent change in demeanor. He was the first to admit that the last few days were filled with more snarls and outbursts than the rest of his five years as alpha all put together. It was a pretty stark contrast to his typical laid-back attitude.

On the other hand, the bonded wolves just regarded him with humor and pity, knowing firsthand what a strong force a true mating call was for a male werewolf.

Of course, the difference for most of them was that their women had welcomed them with open arms and had cemented their bond in a matter of hours. They never experienced the strain Trace was under with Mariam, nor did any of them envy him for it.

Even Randy's struggle with Justine was more mental than a literal game of cat and mouse. While it was happening,

Trace felt bad for him, but now he'd give anything to argue with Mariam face-to-face over their mating bond.

Strain might be an understatement. One look in the mirror told him that his body was simply breaking down under the pressure. Since losing her at the hotel, he hadn't been sleeping, and had no appetite at all. He was losing a lot of weight, most of it probably muscle mass since he wasn't hitting the gym like he usually would, but none of that mattered. All Trace wanted to do was find Mariam.

"What's the word, Trace?" Justin was the youngest member of the team, always eager to prove himself worthy of his place in the pack. The alpha gave him a grim look and pulled up a list of nearby packs on the screen. Another click crossed out the ones that they had already searched, leaving only a small amount on this side of the United States.

"We have searched for my mate at thirteen of the seventeen packs across the states of California, Oregon, Washington, Utah, and Arizona. Mariam's former alpha, Jeremy, informed me that she may have ties to a small pack in Massachusetts. Her mother was originally from there, but she never visited after joining Dark Claw. Mariam's sister is concerned because she has not heard from her since the night she slept in a motel, but I can promise without a doubt that she is alive and well somewhere."

The room of shifters gave him curious looks, each wondering how he could guarantee that she was alive without knowing her location.

He didn't feel like recapping or explaining himself, so Trace clicked to the next slide. It listed the remaining three packs within driving distance of Dark Claw, not counting their own.

His wolf urged him to return home so they could run free in the trees, but Trace reminded him that they needed to wait for their mate. Their runs would be exponentially better with her by their side, and the animal couldn't argue with that.

"We will send three of our men to each pack. Look around without drawing a lot of attention to yourself and remember to provide them with my contact information in case she turns up after you leave."

The men nodded their understanding. He clicked the remote again, and several motels popped up. "Motels are less likely because she will probably run out of money soon. She has no driver's license or phone, just a friend's truck and whatever extra money she had on her."

Trace said the last part through my teeth, intentionally avoiding mentioning the gender of her friend. That little bitch had come between him and his mate for the last time. He couldn't be sure that Mariam had slept with him, which had been the only reason he had spared the boy's life, but Trace definitely wasn't a fan of whatever their friendship entailed. It was just one more thing that would change when she became his in every way.

Jared, another newly appointed wolf, raised a hand in the front row, and Trace nodded at him to speak. "So far, none of the motels have helped a girl who meets your mate's description, but we have given them her photo in case she checks in. Maybe circulating her photo with the other packs might help, too."

His wolf growled his discomfort at the idea, and Trace had to agree with him. His pride had taken a big hit when he had to form a team to search for his mate. It was even more challenging to humble himself to the point of asking other packs for help in finding her. The fact that he had to chase my female across the countryside was demeaning.

Randy stepped in, clearing his throat, and putting a hand on Trace's shoulder. "That won't be necessary, Jared. Giving her picture to humans is one thing, but we don't want to start posting pictures of our alpha's mate on foreign pack lands. This needs to be taken care of as discreetly as possible for the good of our pack."

The elder wolves nodded their agreement with the beta. Trace appreciated him answering the question and making it a pack issue rather than one of his own bruised pride. Jared seemed to accept the response, especially after his alpha nodded approval at his attempt to take initiative.

"If there aren't any more questions, please see Randy to receive your assignment on the way out. We will leave at first light, so get some sleep."

"That goes for you, too, alpha." The oldest member of the team was his uncle. No one else in the room would have dared to issue Trace a directive, but the alpha gave him a nod of agreement. He did need to get more sleep. He would start making stupid mistakes if he wasn't thinking with a clear head.

Trace handed the remote to Randy on his way out, stumbling back to the bedroom of the large rental. The house was just outside the boundaries of Mariam's former pack, allowing him to be there at a moment's notice if she returned.

He tugged his shirt off over his head and tossed it on an armchair, not bothering to put it away properly. He untied his boots and left his pants in a puddle on the floor. Nothing mattered except taking a warm shower, and trying to get some sleep before another day of hunting for Mariam.

Trace let his mind wander and imagined that the water running down his back was Mariam's hands caressing his. He felt his eyes shift, his wolf taking over as his fangs lengthened. He was more than ready to claim Mariam as their mate.

His cock pulsed in the steam, aching for a taste of her pussy. He groaned, thinking about how it would feel to have her squeeze her inner muscles around his shaft. He wanted to have her screaming his name while he pounded himself into her over and over again.

Trace used his hand, taking out his desperation for her on his own body. Between the heat of the shower and the image of her in his bed, it didn't take long for him to come; he cried out in pleasure and frustration as he spilled his seed.

He should be emptying himself into her rather than down the shower drain. If only he had controlled himself and held on to her that first night at the hotel….

But none of that could be helped now. The only thing Trace could do was find her and try to keep his wolf under control, no matter how she tried to bait him.

He grabbed a towel and made quick work of drying himself. He slept naked most nights, and tonight was no exception. The alpha groaned when his dick tented the sheets again, still hungry for the woman he couldn't have tonight.

He turned onto his side, punching the pillow in an attempt to get comfortable. Finally, he fell asleep for the first time since meeting his mate.

It was her laugh that called to him first. She was laughing, probably joking, with another woman. Trace felt himself grin at the relaxed way she interacted with her companion.

Hello, mate, he whispered to her in their shared consciousness. Her reaction to him was already in motion before he even greeted her, as though she could sense his presence before he made himself known. Trace felt her stiffen and her heart rate increase as she walked away from her friend, slowly at first but then in a full-out run.

Mariam alternated between squinting her eyes and looking at the ground, causing him to frown and worry about her safety. Wherever she was, it was dark outside already, and walking around half-blind might cause her to injure herself.

Always running, little wolf. Where are you going in such a hurry?

More jumbling told him that she was climbing stairs, and the next thing that came into focus was a front door. He felt a rush of excitement and strained to see any identifiable information about the place she was living, but there was too much movement.

You're doing that on purpose, He accused her gently. This much jostling and blinking wasn't necessary; she was trying to prevent him from being able to see what she was looking at. His mate was as clever as she was beautiful.

She sighed and moved within the apartment until she stopped at a bedroom. She turned to close the door before settling on a bed alone. Finally, she opened her eyes fully, allowing Trace an unobstructed view of her surroundings.

It was a simple bedroom with a desk and chair, a dresser,

and a single mirror hanging on the wall. Mariam's gaze lowered to the bed, unintentionally showing off her long legs in the shorts she was wearing. He rumbled my approval at her appearance.

How was your day? Trace asked. Randy had made a good point; if she was scared of him, maybe he could solve that problem by showing her he was approachable and that he cared for her. Trace felt her confusion.

My day went really well. How was yours? He knew that the response was probably automatic and polite, but he couldn't help feeling victorious that she answered.

My day was fine. I miss you, and I've been thinking about you. He left out that his most recent thoughts included her spread eagle on his bed and sucking his dick in the shower.

You must be sleeping, she said, changing the subject. *This happened when I was napping earlier.*

I am, he confirmed. *This is the first time I've slept since we met. I would have knocked myself out cold if I knew that it meant I would be able to talk to you.*

Trace felt her frown, but Mariam didn't respond. She picked at her quilt and rolled the stray pieces of fuzz in her fingertips. he was relieved to see that wherever she was, at least she was safe in a house rather than living outdoors, but now that he could talk to her, he could make sure she had everything she needed.

Do you need any money?

She stilled at the question. He felt the thoughts shift in her mind as she tried to guess his motive in offering to help her. It was entertaining to witness her debating different possibilities and still be unable to land on a definite answer.

I want to know so I can send you some. Maybe to a bank

account, or I could drop it off at a neutral location. I just want you to have what you need.

Her mind probed his, trying to see if what he offered came with any tricks, but his intentions were pure. He wouldn't try to pull a fast one on her, even if he had to ask Randy to restrain him with a straight jacket.

She giggled at the image of the alpha tied to a chair so he couldn't meet her while she went to collect a check.

I don't need anything but thank you.

Her answer was enough to make him curious, too. *Really? How much money did your friend give you?*

She hesitated again, and Trace felt her reluctance to start another argument. Her desire to have a comfortable relationship with him made him smile.

Whether she wanted to believe it or not, their mating bond was affecting her, too, and giving her a push to submit that wasn't there before. According to the mated males in his pack, the instinct would increase exponentially after biting and bedding her.

I got a job.

His smile disappeared as he stewed over that new bit of information. With a job, she had access to more funds and could go into hiding even longer. Her ability to escape him this long was impressive, Trace had to give her that, but this wasn't a game. This was their lives she was messing with.

Slowly, a new realization dawned on him. *If you have a job, you must be staying with another pack. No human employer would hire you with the few items you left with.*

Not all jobs require documentation, Trace. Not if you know the right people.

The right people? Who the hell did she know outside of

her community? He pushed those questions aside when he realized that, for the first time, she had called him by his name.

Trace couldn't help it. Hearing his name on her lips brought forth a whole new set of fantasies. He imagined her whimpering his name as he forced his dick into her cunt from behind. Her screams of pleasure and pain mixed together. It was more than enough to make him rock hard again.

And then he remembered that he wasn't alone. Mariam was with him, seeing the same lewd display. He felt her shock and… something else. Her arousal filled his senses. The idea of him fucking her was turning her on, too.

He watched as her hand traced the hem of her shirt before dipping lower into her shorts. His animal growled a warning to her.

No! The female's responses belong to us! The aggressive command came straight from his wolf.

Mariam's hand faltered, from embarrassment or obedience, Trace wasn't sure. As much as he wanted to forbid her from masturbating, having that release in the shower was also the only thing getting him through the time they were apart. It felt wrong to say she wasn't allowed to indulge in something he had done only moments before falling asleep.

But his wolf didn't care. Their kind was full of double standards for males and females when it came to mates. The males set the rules, and the females obeyed, even when it was unfair. End of story.

Mariam waited, listening as he argued with his wolf, trying to reason with him, but he wasn't having it.

It doesn't matter, she said. *I'm going to bed.*

As she stood, Trace caught a glimpse of her face in the mirror, and it made his wolf howl with approval. All his anger evaporated with the new distraction. The alpha couldn't blame him; she was as gorgeous as ever. He stared at her for as long as he could, and then the whole room went dark.

Chapter 8

I learned that the trick to avoiding Trace was to go to sleep at the same time as him. True, he had turned up a time or two in my dreams, but we were not able to have the long, disturbing conversations that we shared when one of us was awake. For some reason, when neither of us was conscious, our connection wasn't as strong.

That only lasted for a few days until he caught on to what I was doing and started sleeping on an opposite schedule.

The real problem was that I had already blabbed to him about having a job, so one day he intentionally fell asleep during regular business hours to see where I was working.

Fortunately, I had anticipated that and was one step ahead of him. As soon as I felt his presence, I put on some dollar store sunglasses and squinted my eyes until I could barely see through the lenses.

That's not going to work. I'll still figure it out, he said smugly.

Before I could respond, one of the kindergarten students approached me to help them tie their shoes.

"Ms. Ella, why did you put those dark glasses on your face?" the child asked, pointing to my sunglasses with innocent curiosity.

I groaned, hating that the child was giving away so much information but knowing at the same time that it wasn't their fault. I felt Trace chuckle at my dilemma as I knelt to tie the loose laces.

Ms. Ella, huh? And here I thought your name was Mariam. His voice dripped with sarcasm, which did nothing to hide the delight he felt at receiving the new information.

Nope, that's my sister. Maybe you should go bother her instead. I had meant it as a jab, but the idea had some merit to it. Ella wanted a mate, and so did Trace. Obviously. If he mated with Ella, they could both be happy and leave me to the life I was living.

NO.

I scowled at Trace's reaction, annoyed that he wasn't even going to hear me out and consider it.

I can hear your thoughts, so you don't need to explain it to me, Mariam. And I don't need any time to consider it because it's a stupid idea. Ella isn't my true mate. You are. End of story.

I huffed and went to help another student who needed to wash the glue off their hands. Overhead, the lunch bell rang.

So, you're working at a school, not a preschool or daycare. No human school would hire you without at least a social security card, so it must be a pack school. And there are only so many packs that I haven't searched yet, Mariam. His smooth voice distracted me from my task, causing the child I was helping to complain. *You should prepare to see me soon, mate. I'll be coming for you shortly.*

His confidence annoyed me, so I played the only card I had. *Don't you think I'd be able to see your plans and all your surroundings if you tried to hop on a plane to come and get me? If you had any clue where I was, I would already know it because of this connection.*

I felt Trace's breath catch in his chest. I tried not to let my emotions leak through, but I was proud of regaining the stronger position in our exchange.

He was silent for a few minutes. His thoughts raced by in his mind fast enough to make me dizzy. Between that and the children running around me, it was difficult to keep track of everything he was considering.

Unfortunately, I think you're right, little wolf. The sadness in his voice caused me to freeze in my tracks. I felt his emotion as strongly as he did.

Therefore, although I have thoroughly enjoyed our time together and love sharing this bond, I'm going to have to block you out until we are mated and sealed. There's not a chance in hell I'm letting you get away just because you're a clever she-wolf.

I frowned at his words. There's a way to block this? I could have been blocking this the whole time?

Trace chuckled. *It's one of the benefits of being well-versed in werewolf law, I guess. But just so you know, Mariam, when I find you -and I will find you- the first thing I'm going to do is put you over my knee and spank your ass raw for putting us through this.*

My cheeks flamed at the threat, and my hand instinctively traveled behind me to shield my backside. The idea of him putting me across his lap was humiliating. Maybe I had gone too far. There had to be another way to talk him out of trying to find me. *Trace?*

There was no answer, and I could feel that his presence was gone. I removed the sunglasses, unsure if I should celebrate.

On the one hand, I had gotten him out of my head and protected my own thoughts, but on the other, now I wouldn't know if he was coming to search Tumblewild. I wasn't sure which was worse.

"This is delicious, Ella," Gabe said as he reached for more of the chicken alfredo I made for our evening meal. Without entering Trace's mind each night, I was getting more sleep over the past few weeks, and I had a lot more energy to help around the house.

It was Saturday, and Gabe had to put in a few extra hours at work, so I decided to scrub the small apartment clean and cook a meal from scratch.

Chicken alfredo was one of the only things I knew how to make, other than simple breakfast food. It felt good to watch him enjoy it. He seemed stressed lately due to a lot of key council members being absent.

I had been at Tumblewild for about a month, and each day I was another day closer to having to leave for good. But before I started planning my next destination, there were a few things I wanted to ask Gabe.

"I'm glad you like it," I said, offering him another roll. He accepted it gladly. I swallowed hard, knowing that this would be the best time to ask what had been weighing on my mind all day. "Gabe, you know a lot about werewolf law, right?"

My friend nodded slowly, mouth full of noodles and sauce. He regarded me carefully, sensing that I was going to ask something serious. "Well, I was wondering… I heard before that chosen mates… you know, not true mates… that they can't hear each other's thoughts and that the males aren't as possessive. Is that true?"

"Yeah, that's the catch, right? If your mate is a gift from the goddess, you get all those things, plus mind-blowing sex, a feeling of belonging, boosted fertility."

He listed the reasons like he was marking off a checklist. I had to hide a grin because it was the first time Gabe had been able to say the word sex without turning red. He had become a lot more comfortable around me over the past few months, even allowing for the occasional hug.

"Yeah, I got it. But if someone doesn't want those things, would it be possible to mate with another wolf and break the true mate bond?"

He looked at me like I was crazy.

"Yes. It's happened before, but I don't think it's very common. Like, at all. Why would anyone settle for a regular mating when you already know who your true mate is?"

I rolled my eyes. "You're a guy, so you'd never understand. Being on the female end of a true mating is horse shit. Regular werewolf men are bad enough with their bossiness and controlling ways, but who wants some egomaniac in their head, ready to punish them for breaking some stupid arbitrary rule?"

Gabe set his roll down and sighed. "Well, first off, I would be curious to know who in Tumblewild has been bossing you around and giving you rules. You aren't a mated she-wolf, and you haven't even met our alpha or beta, so there's no one here who has that kind of authority over you."

I shifted uncomfortably in my seat and looked away. My wolf whined and rolled over onto her back, ashamed of what Gabe thought of our choices.

"Oh. Um, do you have a...*boyfriend*...or something, Ella? Does he know that you're living here with me?" He emphasized the word boyfriend to try to make his question obvious. He didn't need to; what he was asking me was crystal clear. He wanted to know if I was fucking someone.

"Not here, no. But I had boyfriends back home. I don't believe in the whole chastity thing, which is another reason I wouldn't want a true mate. I wouldn't want to be tied to just one man. I want my freedom."

Horror crossed Gabe's face before he could mask it. "Ella, I'm not trying to judge you. I think it's great that you're happy, but you are seriously overestimating what male werewolves are willing to put up with. Even regular chosen mates wouldn't handle something like that very well."

"Would you?" I asked, entirely serious.

"No way," he answered flatly. "Just thinking about my mate looking at another male is enough to make me want to punch someone. And I'd absolutely send her over my knee if she gave another man any attention."

"Okay, fine. But even if I had to be monogamous with a

chosen mate, I wouldn't have the increased possession and the mind-reading. So that's better than the other option, right?" I felt like I was grasping at straws. Gabe reached over and patted my shoulder awkwardly.

"It's going to be okay, Ella," he said, frowning. "Why are you so worried about true mate stuff all of a sudden? It's not like you've met one here, have you?"

Gabe set his roll down. His brow furrowed until realization filled his eyes. I could almost feel the moment he finally put two and two together.

"What, Gabe? It's not like I'm in a strange pack trying to escape a bad, true mate bond or anything, right?" I laughed bitterly, not daring to make eye contact with him.

"Hey," he said, his voice much softer now. He placed a finger under my chin and forced me to look back at his face. "It's going to be okay. If you are positive that this guy is bad for you, I'll try and help you find a different mate. There are lots of wolves in this town who would love to bond with you. And if you couple with someone in Tumblewild, you can become a permanent member of the pack."

That was precisely my line of thinking, but I was still hesitant. "But won't they care that I'm not... you know... a virgin?"

Gabe sighed and picked up his roll again. "I'm not one for deceiving people, but maybe don't lead with that? Let them get to know you, and after a while, they probably won't even care."

I quirked an eyebrow at him. My wolf looked perplexed, too. *Any male who doesn't care would not make a worthy mate,* she declared. I rolled my eyes at her.

"Okay, fine. They'll probably still care, but as long as you promise to be exclusive with them from now on and not share any of the gory details, a good mate will leave it in the past."

I had to smile at his confidence because inside, I had none of my own.

———

Gabe wasted no time compiling a list of potential bachelors for me to meet. He woke me up early the following day to discuss some of his ideas. It was cute how excited he was, and I appreciated that he wanted me to stay in Tumblewild. Other than missing a few people in Dark Claw, I enjoyed living with him a lot more than when I was roommates with Ella.

"Are any of them gay?" I mumbled, reaching for a cup of coffee. "If my mate was gay, we could both see people on the side, and he wouldn't care what I was doing."

He looked at me, confused. "If a male in our pack was gay, he'd just mate with another male. This type of situation probably wouldn't interest him at all."

I sighed. He had a point there. "So, how did you choose these guys?"

"They're good wolves, and they haven't seemed eager to go find their true mates," he said. "We're going to have a pack run tomorrow night, and I might ask a couple of them to stop by here afterward if that sounds good to you."

"Wow...so this is really going to happen, huh?" There wasn't a point in drawing it out any longer, so I wasn't sure why a feeling of dread was building in my stomach. At least this way, I'd get a chance to know them before binding myself to one of them forever.

I sat next to Gabe at the kitchen table when his phone dinged with a message.

Some of the stress that he had been carrying around melted off his shoulders as he read it, piquing my curiosity, "Good news?" I asked.

"Very," he said, shoving it back in his pocket. "Our beta and a few of the council members will be back from their business trip today. There's a ton of pack business that we've been putting off without them, and their return will take a lot of the pressure off me."

He gave me an apologetic smile. "Unfortunately, it also means that we're going to have to cut this short because I need to prepare their offices. They've already taken off and should be landing in Flagstaff in about an hour. But we'll do this tonight, okay? Promise."

"Is there anything I can do?" I asked, standing to follow him to the door and grabbing my keys from the hook.

Gabe nodded. "Sure. The big-wigs love having snacks from the bakery available when they arrive, so if you want to pick up the order and drop it off at town hall, that'd be great. Linda said it should be ready in about ten minutes, so you can head over there now."

Happy to take the task off his hands, I followed him out the door, and we walked together to the small parking lot. I smiled as I considered my new life, feeling much more positive than the evening before.

The possibility of getting to stay in Tumblewild with Gabe made me see that maybe not everything was ruined when I met Trace. Perhaps being truly mated to him was the motivation I needed to leave my old pack behind and start a new life.

———

"Hi, Linda," I said, greeting the town hall receptionist and peeking my head around the boxes of pastries in my hands. "Gabe asked me to pick these up for the council members arriving today. Do you know where he wants them"

Linda nodded and pointed to a door on the left. "We usually set them out in that conference room. The members just arrived, but they won't start their meeting for about ten more minutes. Would you mind setting them out on the trays in there? There's a large ceramic stand and a few smaller serving dishes. The drinks and glasses were set up this morning, so no need to do anything with those."

"Sure, no problem." I walked sideways through the door, trying my best to balance the boxes and not trip over my own feet. Somehow, I managed to set out the food and napkins with a few minutes to spare. When Gabe entered the room, he gave me a grateful look that made me feel like a million bucks.

"Thanks for your help, El. If you want to stick around for a few minutes, I'll introduce you to our beta. Or one of our betas, I should say. We have two, a mated couple. If you decide to petition for pack membership, he would be the one to approve it if our alpha hasn't returned, so it might be a good idea to say hello."

I nodded, suddenly nervous. The only beta I had ever known was Neil, and he was kind of an asshole.

Gabe gave my hand a squeeze. "Don't worry. Our beta was an outsider, and he had to petition for membership, too, so he knows how you feel. And if the mating ceremony goes forward, it will be completely painless."

"Mating ceremony? Are you planning on declaring a mate, Gabe?" A sandy-haired werewolf grinned at him from the doorway.

Gabe smiled back politely and gestured to where I was standing across the room. "You haven't met Ella Landis yet, Randy. She's the one I contacted you about, remember? She's visiting for a few months, but she might like to apply for pack membership at some point."

The smile on my face quickly turned to a frown as our eyes met, causing Randy to do the same. He looked familiar, but I couldn't remember where I'd seen him before.

Realization dawned on him first, causing him to slam the door shut and reach for his phone.

"Are you okay, Randy?" Gabe frowned, sending him a look of concern. "Is something wrong?"

And that's when I remembered. He was one of the wolves in the Feldman Hotel when I first met Trace. And I had seen him in my dreams through Trace's eyes. But if he was the beta of Tumblewild, that meant...

I turned to Gabe; my eyes filled with panic. "You have to get me out of here," I begged. "Please, I'll explain everything, but I need you to help me."

Chapter 9

Randy held the phone a good foot away from his face as Trace yelled at him through it. He didn't need to put it on speakerphone; Gabe and I could hear every word from where we stood across the room.

"You're telling me she's at Tumblewild? Is that what you're fucking telling me, Randy? She's standing in my fucking conference room while I am interviewing packs in Massachusetts, trying to find anyone who has seen or heard from her?"

The ranting went on like that for a few more minutes. The beta made no attempt to answer Trace's questions because there really wasn't anything else to say. Gabe's hand rubbed my back in small circles, trying to comfort me and still attempting to understand what was going on.

"Put her on the phone this fucking instant!"

Randy pushed away from the wall he was leaning on and walked toward me, phone outstretched. I shook my head, not wanting to be on the receiving end of whatever else he was going to start screaming about.

"You know Trace?" Gabe asked, turning to me.

"Who the fuck is that?" Trace's voice dipped a few octaves

when he heard Gabe's voice.

I sighed and took the phone. "Hi, Trace," I said, not sure what else to say. I'd say pretty much anything to get his attention away from Gabe.

"Hello, Mariam." His voice sounded like nails on toast, but at least he wasn't yelling anymore.

I frowned and hit the speakerphone button. It was difficult to hear him now that he was speaking at a regular volume, but I wasn't going to risk my hearing by putting it up to my ear in case he went off the rails again.

"You sound well-rested," Trace said. "Have you enjoyed getting to know your new pack mates this past month?"

I frowned at his change in tone, wondering if it was a trick. "Actually, yes. I'm not an official pack member. I'm just visiting, but Gabe and I were talking about ways to make it permanent."

"Oh, you and Gabe were talking…that's *great*." I heard him throw something heavy in frustration, even though his tone remained even. "Well, you and Gabe won't have to worry about that anymore, Mariam. I'm the fucking alpha of Tumblewild, so when our mating bond is complete, you will sure as fuck be a member. And a rather important one at that."

I closed my eyes slowly. It was taking me time to process everything, but that was probably due to the shock of it all. Trace wasn't just a council member; he was the mysterious alpha who had been gone since before I arrived. And of course, if we were mated, Tumblewild would become my new home.

"I didn't know this was your pack, Trace. If I did, I sure as hell wouldn't have tried to hide out here."

"Yeah, it never occurred to any of us that you might be there," he said, sighing. "But I thought you knew who I was. You knew my name and…well, it doesn't matter now. I'll be there as soon as I can." His voice teetered on the brink of exhaustion.

"Anything else you want to say, boss, or should I just take it from here?" Randy asked, grabbing the phone from my outstretched hand.

"Do you think you can manage to take it from here, Randy? Can I trust you to babysit my mate until I can catch a flight back to Flagstaff?"

I winced, sympathizing with the beta who didn't deserve the harsh criticism.

"I guess you probably can," he said slowly. "Seeing as how I wasn't the one who let her get away in the first place."

The phone erupted with a string of expletives from Trace, but Randy didn't look concerned. He ended the call and ran his fingers through his hair, his eyes bouncing from Gabe to me and landing on Gabe's hand, still rubbing circles on my upper back.

"If you want to keep all your appendages intact, you should probably stop touching her like that. Just a friendly warning before our alpha returns."

It turned out that a direct flight from Boston to Flagstaff was over six hours of airtime. Add that to the drive time to get to the airport and the two hours Trace had to wait in the airport for a flight, and his estimated time of arrival in a best-case scenario was sometime after seven in the evening.

Randy was worried that I would try to bolt if one of us left the room for any reason, so the first three hours of waiting consisted of him leaning against the door and Gabe and I whispering to each other in the corner.

If Gabe had a single spiteful bone in his body, he would have been pissed at me for keeping so many secrets from him. Instead, he listened to my story and asked questions to understand my motivation for coming to Tumblewild in the first place. He sighed and shook his head when everything was out on the table. I held my breath, waiting for his judgment.

"It's not what I would have done, but I can understand that you felt the need to run and hide from Trace. I'm glad you ended up here with me instead of with a psychopath or something."

"That's the nicest thing anyone's ever told me," I said, only half-joking. I reached forward to hug him and thank him for not hating me.

From his space near the door, Randy cleared his throat and shook his head, not taking his eyes off the game he was playing on his phone.

Gabe released me and scooted away to put some space between us. I turned my attention toward the door, specifically focusing on the beta.

"Um…Randy?" I asked, squirming slightly.

"Yes, Mariam Hinder slash Ella Landis slash the future Mrs. Trace Everett?"

So, Trace's last name was Everett. I stored that piece of information away. "I need to use the restroom, please."

Randy didn't even look up from his game. "Nope. Not going to happen."

"I'm not sure if I can hold it for another five hours,

Randy."

"Then things are going to get a little more interesting in here." His tone made it clear he wasn't interested in negotiating.

Gabe growled low, which caused Randy and me to both turn and look at him with surprise. "Come on, Randy," he said. "Even prisoners get to use the bathroom. Let her go. She's not going to run anywhere, right?" He turned to me for confirmation, and I nodded. There was no getting out of this mess.

"Oh, is that right? I don't think you know Ms. Whoever-she-is as well as you think you do, Gabe," Randy grumbled. "That's what the council had been doing this whole month, if you didn't know. We have been going on a crazy wild goose chase looking for her. But does it bother her that you've had twice the workload, and Trace has been a complete lunatic to the point that none of us want to deal with him right now? You bet it doesn't. She wasn't interested in even hearing him out or trying to make it work. She ducked her tail and left him standing in a parking lot. If her scent was any indication, she probably went back to fuck her boyfriend on the same night she got another motherfucker killed for jumping on his dick."

My wolf whined, not wanting to hear any more. I was beginning to like Randy about as much as I liked Neil back home. Gabe's growl intensified.

"Do you really think that our alpha is going to appreciate you saying those things about his mate? When he gets back here-"

"When he gets back here, he can say it all to her face himself," Randy finished.

Gabe stood up and helped me to my feet. "Randy, I'm trying to understand what you've gone through this last month and be sympathetic to all the shit you had to endure as our beta, but I'm taking her to the bathroom. You can come with us if you want."

Randy's gaze turned to steel as he looked Gabriel up and down. Finally, he stood and opened the door. "She has four minutes, and then I'm coming in there."

The beta called to Linda and motioned for her to join us. She was going to be my babysitter while the men waited just outside, but I couldn't care less. I really had to go.

"So…this has been an interesting day for you, I bet," she said from outside the stall.

I laughed at her attempt to make a joke, but I was also thinking about what Randy had said back in the conference room. Did Trace actually feel that way about me? I felt my stomach sink at the thought of him being angry like that and thinking so little of me, which was surprising. What was wrong with me? Why did I suddenly care what Trace Everett thought about me?

Because he is our mate and our alpha. We are accountable to him, my wolf reasoned. As serious as her words were, she was also overflowing with excitement with the knowledge that Trace was coming home to us. *Do you think he will want to go on a run tonight?* Her voice sounded so hopeful.

I shrugged, not wanting to rain on her parade but at the same time guessing that the likelihood of Trace wanting to go on a run was next to zero.

I was washing my hands when Randy walked into the women's restroom, Gabe in tow rolling his eyes. "See," he said. "I told you she wasn't going anywhere."

"Yeah, yeah. I get it. She's here." Randy rolled his shoulders and looked uncomfortable. "Can you give us a minute, Linda?"

The receptionist smiled and gave me a wink before slipping out the door.

"Listen," Randy started. "The things I said--"

I held up my hand to stop him. "It's okay, Randy. I know we got off on the wrong foot, and it makes sense for you not to have the best impression of me. For what it's worth, I didn't want to hurt your alpha. I just wanted to continue living my life. To me, he was just some random shifter who was weirdly obsessed with me. I know you won't believe this, but I honestly never wanted to mate with anyone. Ever."

I took a deep breath, giving him the chance to speak, but he was too busy listening, as was Gabe. "I'm not going to explain my sexual history to you. It's not any of your business. And if Trace has a problem with my past, he's probably better suited for someone else anyway."

I dried my hands on a few paper towels and waited for the men to lead me back to the conference room, but neither of them moved. Instead, Randy began to smile, and he even laughed a little bit.

"Better suited for someone else, huh? No, I'd say you two are just about perfect for each other."

The energy in the room changed considerably after my little speech. Randy abandoned his post by the door and joined us. We shared a late lunch --or was it dinner?-- of pastries and cold coffee. The beta pulled a flask from his jacket and poured a little booze into each of our cups. It wasn't nearly enough to get us drunk, but it almost served as an unspoken warning: we would need the extra ounce of liquid courage when the alpha arrived.

We were chatting, with Randy sharing funny stories about Trace, when Gabe cleared his throat, causing us to shift our attention to him.

"Would our alpha be upset to learn that Ella- er, Mariam- has been staying at my apartment with me?"

The smile dashed off of Randy's face, and it was replaced with a tired look. He brought his hand to his face and massaged his forehead like he was suddenly suffering from a painful headache. "Yes, Gabe. That's probably something that would be concerning to him. I had forgotten that those were your living arrangements."

My cheeks flushed. "Nothing happened," I rushed to explain. "Gabe has two bedrooms, and I didn't have a place to stay. That's the only reason he invited me over."

"You don't have to explain things to me, sweetheart. I'm completely rational, and I understand the situation. You might want to ease Trace into that conversation on another day when he has had a chance to sleep. And eat."

"What do you mean?" I asked, feeling an inexplicable tug of concern.

Randy let out a low whistle. "You really don't know what you're in for. Trace has lost at least thirty pounds this month, maybe more, and he only sleeps in half-hour increments, usually in the car. When I tell you he's on edge, I'm not exaggerating."

My heart sank to think of him in such a state. I couldn't imagine what his tall frame would look like with thirty pounds missing considering he wasn't overweight to begin with. His body was solid, like a wall, but would he look weaker now? I guess in a few hours, I'd be able to see for myself. Randy scooted his chair back and stood up.

"C'mon. Let's get your stuff out of Gabe's place before Trace gets back. We should have enough time to get there and back before he lands."

We both nodded and followed him out. I pulled my keys from my purse, earning myself a wary look from Randy. "I'm exhausted, Mariam," he complained. "So help me, if you try to escape in that fucking truck--"

I sighed and tossed the keys to him. "Let's go," I answered, taking both his and Gabe's hand. "I'll sit in the middle."

The offer seemed to reassure the beta, and he drove us there in a much better mood. When we entered the apartment, Gabe and I exchanged glances as we walked by the kitchen table. It was hard to believe that only a few hours ago we were sitting there together talking about-

"Hey, do you still have the list of potential mates? You know, the list of single Tumblewild males?" I asked Gabe, full-on deadpan. "You promised we would discuss it tonight."

Randy blinked, trying to process my words, but Gabe cracked up instantly. He laughed until tears were forming in the corners of his eyes.

"I don't think I even want to know what you're talking about, but it's good that you're getting this sort of thing out of your system now," Randy said. "Let's just get your stuff and get out of here."

Packing was easy. The only items I had were the things

from Patrick's house, the Walmart blanket, and the charger for the crappy cellphone I purchased with my first paycheck at the school. *The school.* Tomorrow was Monday. I was supposed to clock in at the school at seven-thirty sharp. The kindergarteners and teachers were counting on me to be there.

My hesitation caused me to stop packing, which frustrated Randy. "What is it now?" he asked.

"My job. I'm supposed to TA in the kindergarten room in the morning."

He sighed. "You'll have to take that up with your mate, Mariam, but something tells me he isn't going to be sending you to school in the morning. I'm sure he can write you a note or something."

I scowled at him. This was serious. The classes were crowded, and there wasn't enough support staff to cover as it was. I shook my head, dropping my bag on the floor. "If he's going to try and prevent me from working, there's no need for me to move out of here."

"Mariam," Gabe said, trying to reason with me. "You were going to leave that job in a few months anyway, remember? They knew when they hired you that you weren't a permanent employee or even a pack member."

"Well, that settles it," Randy said, bending to pick up my bags. "Let's get out of here. Trace will be landing any minute, and we need to be waiting for him at the town hall when he gets there. I'm not going to get my ass chewed out again today."

We drove back to the town hall, my two bags in tow. Once again, I found myself in the middle of the front seat. Our timing was perfect. Trace's call came through as soon as

Randy cut off the engine.

"Hey," Randy answered. "Yeah, I know…. she's here…. yeah, I can do that. Bye."

I was a little surprised to only get one side of the conversation. Trace must be in a better mood, or maybe his throat was just sore from all the yelling earlier.

"He wants me to take you to the house and wait for him there." Randy started the engine again and was about to put the car in gear when Gabe and I looked at each other and burst out laughing.

"Does he want Gabriel to wait at his house, too?" I asked between gasps, imagining the comedy that would occur if Trace found the three of us sitting at his dining room table.

Randy hid his smile, but not fast enough. "You. Out," he said, pointing at Gabe.

Not caring what Randy said, I gave my first friend, my best friend, in Tumblewild a hug goodbye. "Thanks for not letting me be homeless," I whispered.

"Thanks for not stabbing me in my sleep," he answered, giving me one more reassuring squeeze.

"For fuck's sake," Randy grumbled.

Gabe climbed out of the truck with a final wave, leaving Randy and me alone together.

We drove in silence for a little while, but finally, the beta spoke. "You know that's going to have to end, right?"

I didn't answer, choosing to ignore the question and focus on the road ahead. I hoped Randy was wrong, but he knew Trace best. Chances were, he was all too right about my friendship with Gabe being as good as over.

Chapter 10

"Justine!" Randy started hollering the poor woman's name as soon as we stepped inside the expansive alpha house. I quickly slipped out of my shoes, not wanting to track in any dirt. The living room was huge, large enough that a smaller pack might host meetings in it. I left Randy's side to take a better look at the backyard through the oversized glass windows, but he caught my arm quickly.

"I don't think so," he warned. "If you want a tour, you're going to have to wait for the big guy. He should be here in about twenty minutes. Maybe even sooner if he's giving the driver as much hell as I think he is."

I shrugged, not wanting to show how much his suspicion hurt my feelings. It stung that Randy didn't trust me to even go to the other side of the living room after spending all day together. I thought we were starting to get along.

"Justine! Where are you?" The beta resumed his search, one hand securely wrapped around my wrist.

"You must have left your manners in California, Wolfman." A short female werewolf emerged from the kitchen. She had a luxurious mane of red curls and bright blue eyes. She sounded angry, but her face lit up when she saw Randy. She looked like she was going to smother him with hug him but stopped short when she saw me. "Is this her? Are you Mariam?"

I nodded, not sure who she was. *She must be family to our mate. Her scent is similar to his.* My wolf tilted her head and watched with interest. The woman ran to me, throwing her arms around my middle in a hug so fierce, it knocked the wind out of me.

"I'm Justine, as you could probably guess. This oaf was screaming it loud enough that you'll never forget it now." She released me and stuck out her tongue at the pack's beta before grinning and pulling him in for a kiss.

I stared at them, too shocked to be embarrassed at their intense display of affection.

"I've missed you, troublemaker," Randy growled just loud enough for me to hear. "Wait until I get you to bed. You won't know what--"

Justine elbowed him and gestured to me. The awkwardness was quickly overriding the shock, and I had to look away. "Look, you've embarrassed her. What am I going to do with you?" She huffed and pouted, but it was clearly just for show.

"I can think of a few things you could do with me," Randy answered, his wolf taking over a little, causing his eyes to glow. "But the question really is, what am I going to do with you? Have you behaved while I was gone?"

The female wolf dismissed him with a wave of her hand. "If I didn't, I sure as hell wouldn't be telling you about it." The response flamed her mate's fire, which seemed to be her goal. He flashed his teeth at her.

Mom would have never, not in a million years, spoken to

my father like that. What happened to mates having to be submissive and obedient? I thought that was a universal experience for female werewolves.

"Come on! I have so much to show you. And we have a lot to talk about," Justine said, turning her attention back to me and grabbing me by the hand. Randy relented, releasing his grip when it was replaced by his mate's.

He growled at her enthusiasm, causing her to roll her eyes. "What's wrong with you, Randy? The girl needs to get settled in her new home, and I'm the one who knows everything there is to know about her mate."

"She's not leaving my sight until Trace gets back," he said. Justine started to complain, but Randy was firm. "It's not up for discussion, Justine, so drop it."

In a show of reluctant obedience, Justine uncrossed her arms and took us each by the hand to lead us into the kitchen.

"Fine. I guess the tour and gossip will have to wait," she said apologetically to me.

Her mate narrowed his eyes. "And I'll not have you interfering and stirring things up for Trace. He's really on edge right now."

"Yeah, yeah," she said, waving her hand dismissively again. "My brother's always on the verge of some kind of breakdown. He does it for the attention, you know?"

So, Trace had a sister. A spunky sister. For some reason, the idea of them growing up together was funny to me. I laughed, earning me a dark look from Randy, too.

"I'm serious, you two. Don't push him too hard right now."

Lights flashed outside, drawing our attention to the

rounded driveway. *Here goes nothing*, I said to my wolf. Even she was a little nervous about seeing Trace again face-to-face.

In no time at all, the front door swung wide open, and Trace Everett filled the doorway. I frowned at the way his face had sunken in from the weight loss, but he was still strikingly handsome.

"Not happy to see me, mate?" His eyes flashed as he walked closer. Every inch of him looked like a predator cornering his prey.

"I just…you just look different," I stammered, not wanting to offend him. "You don't look well."

"I've been better," he agreed through clenched teeth. "But don't worry, I'm going to take all my frustration out on your hide, and then I'll be good as new."

He lunged for me, grabbing me by the arm so fast that I didn't have a chance to run. I let out a yelp, and my wolf darted for cover, cowering in the corner. Justine shoved his shoulder hard, but that only caused him to yank me closer, pulling me right up against his chest.

"Can't you see she's terrified? You're acting like a fucking asshole, Trace," she said. Her brother looked down at me, his brown eyes searching my face.

"Are you scared of me, Mariam?" His voice took on a different quality when he wasn't ready to burst at the seams. He sounded almost…empathetic.

He was a huge werewolf, at least twice my size, and he was spewing threats about beating me to death. Of course, I was terrified.

I didn't answer, confident that a response like that would set him off again.

"See? She's too worried to even answer your question. You've been searching every pack in the country with a fine-tooth comb, and you didn't bother to stop and wonder why she doesn't want to be found," Justine argued, stepping between us. "Until you can be a decent mate to this poor girl, she's staying with me."

"No fucking way." Trace and Randy responded in unison.

"Yes, way."

I cleared my throat and tried to pull myself away from Trace, but he wasn't letting me go. "I don't want to ruin your…reunion with your mate, Justine. I can just stay in a guest bedroom or something," I offered.

Trace's growl shook my whole body. The empathetic werewolf was long gone. "You're my mate, and you are going to sleep in our room, Mariam. And if you want to discuss this further, we'll do it in private."

"I think that's our cue to get lost, Justine," Randy said, planting a firm hand on her back and leading her out of the kitchen. She looked like she was going to protest more, but Randy gave her a swift slap on the butt, and she relented.

"We'll talk more tomorrow, Mariam," she promised. "And you! Be nice to her!" She glared at Trace and pointed an accusatory finger at him as she left.

The kitchen felt unnaturally quiet in Justine's wake.

"Are your items already upstairs?" Trace's voice was smooth and calm again, giving me emotional whiplash.

"No." I pointed to the two bags he had ignored by the door, and his eyebrows raised a notch.

"Those are the only things you brought with you? How did you manage to survive for a month like that?"

Not wanting to argue or further endanger Gabe's life, I

shrugged and pulled back to get a better look at him. This time, he released me, and I was able to slip out of his strong arms.

"You look tired." It was an understatement. Bags had formed under Trace's eyes that looked as deep as caverns, and his skin was an ashy grey.

"It's been a rough month, but it was worth it." He gave me a ruthful smile, and I had to look away from the twinkle in his eyes.

"You should get some rest," I suggested, walking around him to grab my bags.

"I agree. We should go to bed," Trace retorted. My mouth went dry at the idea that we would be sharing the same room, let alone the same bed. Fear must have flashed across my face again because his voice was filled with concern when he spoke.

"Are you really scared of me, Mariam? Do you actually think I would ever hurt you?"

"You just told me you were going to," I pointed out quietly.

"I absolutely did not," he protested. "You're my mate. I would rather die than see you injured."

I gaped at him. Was he losing his mind? "You just said that you were going to beat me to a pulp, and then you lunged at me."

"Well, I might have exaggerated a little bit, but you do need to be punished for running away and for everything that came after. But punishment isn't the same thing as a beating, Mariam. Didn't your father ever discipline your mother?"

"Yeah, he did. And that's one reason I'm not ever going

to have a mate." I felt my courage building again. "I don't need or want someone to 'keep me in line,' as they say."

He laughed a genuine, deep belly laugh. "You might not want it, but you definitely need it. Probably more than any female shifter I've ever met. And here I thought Randy had his hands full with my sister."

"Well, then that settles it. You can go and find a sweet, submissive mate, and I can go on doing whatever the fuck I want. We can both win."

A shadow crossed over his face. "Ah, see, that's where you're wrong, little wolf. I'm ready and willing for the task of taming you. Your fire will make you an asset after I harness it. Plus, I'm sure all that pent-up aggression will come in handy when we are together…in other ways."

I hated him. I really, truly did, and we had only been in each other's presence for less than a day total. What did he think it would be like in thirty years? If we managed to survive living with each other that long, that is.

But it was pointless to argue. I picked up my bags and walked to the staircase.

"Our bedroom is the second door on the right," Trace called out after me. "I expect to see you there, ready for bed when I join you."

My throat burned. I wanted to shout something back downstairs at him, but I resisted. He could expect whatever he wanted from me, but that didn't mean I was just going to roll over and do it.

My wolf shifted uncomfortably as I walked past the room he said was his and tried the handle on another one a few doors down.

I hit the lights and was greeted by a king-sized four-poster bed, a matching dresser, and two side tables. It was much fancier than my room back home, but something told me I wasn't going to be able to enjoy it in peace. Trace would put up such a fuss that it almost wasn't even worth it. But if I did what he demanded, it would set a precedent for him to start ordering all kinds of shit from me. Submit or fight; neither option would be easy.

I dropped my bags on the floor and rifled through them to find the shorts and T-shirt combination I had been sleeping in pretty much every night. Thank goodness Gabe had a washer and dryer in his unit; it would have been much harder to make do with my limited wardrobe if he didn't.

The bedroom had an en suite bathroom, and I used it to brush my teeth and wash my face. I was tempted to take a shower, but I didn't want to be naked if Trace came stomping in.

Exhausted, I turned off the lights and climbed into the bed, loving how plush it was under my hands and knees. I paused, an idea forming in my mind.

Would Trace bother yelling at my wolf for not sleeping in his bed? Or would he just give up and leave her alone? The idea had some merit. It's not like I had a lot of other options.

I threw off my shirt and shorts before I could talk myself out of it and invited my wolf to take over. Her fur sprouted, and our bones set in place, shifting to our animal form. She jumped onto the mattress and circled a few times before settling in on top of the thick comforter.

We had just started dozing off when the sound of doors opening and closing echoed through the hallway. The noise roused my wolf, startling her and causing her to jump down and hide. I felt her tremble when Trace opened our door, and light flooded the room again.

"Mariam? I can see your bags in here, little wolf. You've been caught."

My wolf stayed hidden, not moving a muscle. The floor creaked as he took a few steps inside. His scent was even more intense in my wolf form, and she found some comfort in it. Her tail wagged softly, catching his eye.

"Come on, Mariam. You've stalled long enough. It's time for bed, and I don't care if you walk, trot, or if I need to carry you, you're going to sleep in our room with me."

I mulled over his words. His voice was firm, but it didn't have an edge to it anymore. My wolf mewled at him, happy to comply. If I wanted to stop her from leaving with him, I'd have to force a shift, and then I'd be standing in front of him stark-ass naked.

He led my wolf back down the hall. His suite was furnished with the same type of expensive-looking dark wood, but it was even bigger than the other room. This space was clearly meant for two people: the mated alphas who led the pack. He didn't seem to notice my awe. Instead, he stopped at the tall dresser and removed his cufflinks. He absentmindedly untucked his shirt and made quick work of the buttons. He tossed the garment into a bin, followed in short order by his pants.

I forced my wolf to look away before he could remove his underwear. She gazed longingly at the comfortable mattress, but I wasn't having it. She settled on the plush rug at the foot of the bed next to a large steamer trunk.

Trace chuckled and bent down to scratch behind her ears. "You are quite a beauty, Mariam. In all forms." My wolf rolled onto her back, eager for him to rub her belly.

Traitor. Her display was annoying, but it wouldn't do any good to be mad at her. She was just acting on her instincts. It was her nature to be loving and trusting toward our mate, even if his temper sometimes sent her running for cover.

"Are you really going to sleep like that?" Trace asked, still running his fingers through my course fur. I stared back at him through my wolf's eyes, letting him know that I wasn't budging, either.

"Fine," he said, straightening and walking toward the bed. "Suit yourself."

There wasn't any anger in his voice, which surprised me. He turned off the light and laid down in the dark. The silence in the room was deafening, and I waited, unable to sleep. He seemed to have the same problem as he tossed and turned restlessly.

An hour passed, and then two before he spoke again. "Please," he said. "My wolf won't settle without you. Please join me up here."

My wolf didn't wait for my input. She jumped up onto the bed, and it sagged under her larger-than-human size. For a second, I thought Trace might complain about me not shifting, but he didn't seem to care. In one fluid motion, he tucked her head next to his chest and wrapped an arm around her shoulder.

Within seconds, his breathing evened out, and he was completely gone. I studied him in the light of the moon, enjoying the way the stress had melted away from his features. It wasn't long before a deep, restful sleep claimed me, too.

Chapter 11

It was the sound of snoring that woke me up. My eyes flew open, and I struggled to remember where I was as I took in the strange room around me. And then, I remembered what had happened. I was in Trace's bed, which was undeniably more comfortable than the floor, but came with some drawbacks of its own. Namely, being suffocated by a man with the build of a lumberjack. The crushing weight of his arm and upper body was akin to being encased in a furnace, and the heat was quickly becoming unbearable.

I had shifted back to my human form some time during the night, which meant that in addition to being trapped by Trace's body and alone with him in his bed, I was also completely naked.

I groaned, causing Trace's face to scrunch up in his sleep. I stilled my movements and prayed that I didn't wake him up. With a bit of luck, I might be able to scoot out from under his massive form and leave to find some clothes.

A few seconds later, he went back to snoring. I let out a small sigh of relief and lightly pulled his hand away from where he was gripping my torso. Without warning, he tightened his hold and pulled me deeper into the bed so that

I was completely beneath him. He bared his teeth, and his eyes opened slightly. The glow and dilated pupils said they were all wolf.

None of that phased me because I was too distracted by the hard length of his cock pressed into the dip of my stomach. It felt huge, and it twitched against me like it had a mind of its own.

"Female." He breathed deeply, enjoying the smell of our scents mixed together in the bed. I had to admit, it was intoxicating. The hands that wrapped around my waist started moving. First, his thumbs made small circles, almost teasing me, and then he traveled higher until they rested just below my breasts.

I felt liquid heat form below as I squirmed beneath him. He was so close…. all I needed to do was line him up and push forward to have him lodged inside of me.

The muscles of my pussy flexed, imagining how good it would feel to bare down on him. He growled his agreement as if he could read my thoughts, but his wolf had more pressing matters on his mind.

"My human hasn't claimed you, but that doesn't mean I need to wait, little wolf." He dipped his head lower, nuzzling my neck. The action made my heart race, and I felt my wolf fighting to come to the surface. She wanted to join him for this moment, even if she remained in my body.

I blinked back against the shift, struggling to keep her inside and not lose control. He smelled so good, and my head turned on its own to give him better access to my neck.

The second I felt his teeth sink in, sparks of ecstasy flew in front of my eyes. I might have screamed or made a totally different noise as I struggled to breathe, but there was no pain as he claimed me with his bite.

I felt blood trickle down the side of my neck when he released me. Trace's wolf lapped at it, trying to clean it for me, but I was so strung out on endorphins that I didn't care. I wasn't sure how long it took me to come down from that high, but when my mind cleared, Trace was staring down at me. All signs of his wolf were gone, and his expression was unreadable.

His eyes traveled from mine and lingered on his mating mark. It was probably red and angry if it was anything like some of the other fresh ones I had seen. Werewolves might heal quickly, but mating bites were a somewhat serious injury. That was partly because another werewolf's teeth were responsible for the wound and also because it was so deep in a really delicate place on the body. Unfortunately, the male's bite needed to be that deep and hard. If they didn't pierce the skin so intensely, there wouldn't be a lingering scar to display the bonded status of the female.

But if the way the bite had made me feel was a typical rush, maybe the females weren't getting the raw end of the deal in that exchange like I had always assumed. I had to wonder if sex would be as good as everyone had always said.

Trace's gaze dropped to my lips, and I thought for a minute that he was going to kiss me. I felt torn about the thought. My wolf was moon-eyed and ready to give him a litter of pups, but our humans had barely even had a single civil conversation.

The desire to run and process these feelings alone had me struggling to get away. When I pushed against Trace, he didn't try to keep me pinned.

"Look, Mariam, I'm--"

I held my hand up to stop him from fumbling through an apology. There was no point in laying blame. If either of us was more culpable, it was me anyway. The draw to bite me would have been too much to ask him to overcome in a heated moment like that. I should have been stronger and stopped it from happening.

He frowned at the dismissive gesture but didn't say anything else as I wrapped myself in the sheet and walked to the door. I used part of the end as a sling over my shoulder so that if anyone was in the hallway, they wouldn't see the newly forming scar on my neck.

Fortunately, there was no one to witness my walk of shame, and I was able to quickly shuffle back to my room undetected. Anyone seeing me walk out of Trace's bedroom in a sheet would quickly jump to some embarrassing conclusions.

Thankful to finally be alone, I shut the door and leaned a chair under the handle as a makeshift lock. It wouldn't be enough to stop Trace from getting inside, but it would at least slow him down if he tried to break in.

I wandered over to the mirror and stared at the unrecognizable woman on the other side. Tears welled up in my eyes as I poked the shiny skin, testing to see if it was really there. A few pricks of pain were all that it gave me; by tomorrow, I probably wouldn't even be able to feel it.

My wolf drooped at my tears, torn between wanting to comfort me and not understanding why I wasn't excited to be marked by the attractive alpha. It wouldn't do any good trying to explain my feelings to her. If she could understand, she would already feel the loss with me.

I picked through my clothes until I found my one and only turtleneck. I smiled to myself, thinking about the day I had gone shopping with Ella, and she had insisted that it made me look like Reese Witherspoon from *Sweet Home Alabama*. It absolutely did not, but it did do a pretty good job of covering up the bite mark.

When I was satisfied that no one else would see the affected skin, I pulled on some old, comfortable jeans and grabbed the cheap burner phone that I had been using.

I hesitated, holding it in my hand without dialing. I hadn't called Patrick since I left Dark Claw, but I needed to talk to him. He'd understand my feelings about being bitten by Trace. And at the very least, he'd be thrilled to get his truck back since I was no longer on the run.

It rang a few times before he picked up.

"Hello?" His voice was gruff, not the tone he usually used to speak to me. Of course, he wouldn't recognize the new number. He probably thought I was a telemarketer.

"Hey, it's me." I could feel him melt through the phone, and my own shoulders relaxed, too. Not completely, of course, but enough that the difference was recognizable and comforting.

"Oh, jeez. Are you okay, Mariam? Are you safe?"

"Yeah, I'm as safe as I'm ever going to be," I said, sighing. "He found me."

There was a pause on the line, and I thought for a second Patrick had hung up. Finally, he responded.

"Oh."

"Yeah," I sank to the floor and leaned against the bed. "I have been staying with another pack for about a month, and he showed up here last night."

"But you're okay? He hasn't tried to force you into anything?"

I chewed on my lip, unsure of how to answer that. I couldn't say with conviction that he had forced me into accepting the mating bite. That was probably a surprise for both of us. But Trace was definitely keeping me in his home against my will. My silence must have confirmed Patrick's worst fears.

"I'll kill the fucker," he growled. "Tell me the name of the pack, and I'll be there as soon as I can."

"That's not going to help anything, and you know it. He's an alpha, if you didn't know, and he's only trying to pursue his true mate. If you kill him, you're the one who's going to end up executed...or worse." He started to protest, but I cut him off. "It won't do any good anyway, Patrick. He bit me this morning. I'm screwed."

Patrick sucked in a sharp breath upon hearing that information. The mating bite took this out of the realm of something that could be fixed with brute force. As soon as we had sex and sealed the deal, I would start feeling his feelings, thinking his thoughts, like we did in our dreams but all the time. We were becoming one, and an interruption to that process could kill me, too. Once it was complete and in place, the death of my true mate would undoubtedly be the end of me, if not in body, then in spirit.

I remembered that clearly with my own parents. After mom died, it was like the cancer was a blessing for my dad. He wasn't eating or sleeping anyway. He had almost wasted away to nothing before the chemo had even started taking its toll. I refused to have a death like that; I'd much rather end things on my own first.

As if sensing my thoughts, Patrick growled again. "Don't even think about it, Mare. We will do something to fix this. Maybe some time together will show him that, despite being incredibly hot, you've got a lot of issues."

I snorted at the backhanded compliment. He was trying to make me feel better, and it was working. "I'm not sure how to get your truck back to you. I know driving my old clunker must be a drag."

"That's really the last thing on my mind right now, Mariam," Patrick replied dryly. "Look, don't do anything to piss him off, see if you can block the connection at all if it starts to form, and we'll both try to come up with some solutions. I'm not going to lose you like this. I miss you, Mare."

His voice was so quiet at the end that I almost couldn't hear it. "I miss you too, Patrick. I'll call again soon."

I hung up and set the phone on the floor beside me. I closed my eyes, trying to imagine when I would see Patrick or Lance or anyone else from my normal life again. Maybe Trace would agree to let me visit home, though something told me he would insist on coming with me.

It wasn't going to help to stay in the bedroom all day sulking, especially because I didn't want to give Trace a reason to come and find me. I showered and tidied up the room a little bit by putting away my clothes and straightening the bedsheets.

If Trace had just let me sleep in here, I wouldn't be wearing his bite mark right now. I frowned and wondered if the thought had occurred to him. It was impossible to tell if he regretted what happened, as it was pretty much what he said he wanted. I was now tied to him, without any apparent options for escape.

I stilled at the sound of someone knocking on the door.

"Yes?" I called out.

"Mariam, we need to talk." Trace's voice sounded gruff. Was he irritated again already? That's the last thing I felt like dealing with right now.

"Can we talk later, Trace? I'm tired."

He paused. "You've already been talking to someone else, so there's no reason you can't talk with me."

I frowned. Were the walls really that thin, or was the mating bond already falling in place for him? He had blocked our communication before. Did he know some trick for using it to spy on me now?

Trace tried to turn the doorknob from the hallway and let himself in, but the chair prevented him from doing it. I grinned at his dilemma, pleased that if he was going to be eavesdropping on me, at least he wasn't able to just stroll into my room at any minute.

We will share his room now. My wolf scowled at me, unhappy with my uncharitable behavior toward the alpha. *He should know about our conversations as we will know about his. We are true mates.*

I could feel Trace's uncertainty through the door, almost like he was arguing with his wolf, too.

It wouldn't do any harm to hear him out. It's not like I would be able to leave his house undetected, and at least right now, he wasn't shouting or trying to break the door down. That had to be a step in the right direction. I removed the chair, setting it back on four feet.

Slowly, I turned the knob and opened the door a crack. He was standing in the hallway, looking at me with one eyebrow crooked upward. I felt my breath catch in my throat. He was…gorgeous. More than gorgeous. The man was almost irresistible to look at. I shook my head, trying to discard the unwanted thoughts.

"Are you alright, Mariam?" His voice was soft, and it sounded almost like he genuinely cared. I blinked again, not sure why the thought of him caring suddenly mattered to me.

He frowned at my reaction. Leaning forward, he opened the door wider and welcomed himself inside. He spied the phone on the floor but didn't say anything about it.

"Listen, I'm sorry about what happened this morning. I know you aren't ready for all of this," Trace said, gesturing to himself and me. "The bite wasn't something I planned. My wolf…he isn't the most patient creature, and I've been letting him call the shots too much lately, especially in matters surrounding you…."

Trace was talking, but I was no longer paying attention to the words coming out of his mouth. My eyes were on his chest and shoulders, loving how the shirt he was wearing showed off his muscles.

I reached up and traced the outline of his form lightly with my fingertips. I started at the base of his forearm and drew a line with my finger past his biceps, turning to follow the curve of his collarbone. I snaked down his chest, going lower, lower, until he stopped my hand with his own.

The way he grabbed me broke the trance and startled me out of my aroused state. I felt my wolf near the surface, sure that she was looking through my eyes hungrily at our mate.

"You are a worthy mate," she acknowledged. "My female is pleased with your body, and I am thankful for your dominance."

Trace's eyes flashed, shifting to the wolf at the compliment, and he closed the distance between us. "I will provide everything you need, female. You have my word."

I blinked my wolf away, but the urge to jump in Trace's arms was still there. So, I did.

I straddled him, wrapping my legs around his hips as he used one arm to support me and hold me in place. My lips found his, eager to taste him for the first time. His surprise caused him to hesitate, but soon his mouth softened and opened for me. I used my tongue to search every inch of him, and he did the same, groaning at our passionate exchange.

Trace backed me up against the wall, pinning me there so that his hands were free. Suddenly they were in my hair and on my face. One found the base of my throat, and he applied just enough pressure there to drive me wild. I bucked against him and tried to find some relief for the ache between my legs.

I was getting close to finding my orgasm from the friction I created between us when he stilled. Slowly, he untangled himself from me and stepped away. I reached out, eager to feel his body against mine again, but he moved out of my reach and ran his hands through his hair. His chest was heaving from the encounter, just like mine. I might have taken this rejection more personally in another circumstance, but right now, I just felt confused. *Doesn't he want more?*

"I want a lot more," he said, sighing and answering my unspoken question. "But the reason you feel this way is because of that bite on your neck. Until a few minutes ago, you wanted nothing to do with me, Mariam. I can't take advantage of you like this when your animal is the one in charge."

My breath caught in my throat, and I groaned. He was right; Trace was irresistible. His scent, his body, all of it called to me in a way that it never had before. His claim was slowly evening the playing field between us. I was getting a small taste of how he had felt the last month when I was out of reach.

"What am I going to do?" The question was directed to myself, but since I said it aloud, Trace responded.

"*We* are going to try and take this slow," he said, emphasizing the 'we' in his answer. "Let's get to know each other a little better, and then being mated will feel much more natural for you."

I looked at him with a high level of suspicion and disbelief, causing him to laugh. "I'll admit that I'm not the most patient person, especially when it comes to you, Mariam, but I will be good. My wolf is already mellowing because he was able to mark you. Seeing your unmarked skin and knowing that another male could try and bite you was driving him crazy."

His offer was the best that I was going to get. There wasn't really anything else we could do, so I just nodded and turned to leave.

His fingers brushed against my arm before I could escape. Trace gently turned me so that I was facing him again. His dark eyes softened, and he reached up to touch a loose curl that had fallen out of place.

"You'll never believe this, Mariam, but I do love you. I know you see me as a crazed asshole, but you'll see. I'll provide everything you need."

I brushed his hand aside and turned to leave again, this time with a little more haste. His touch was addicting, and I didn't want to get sucked in again. It wasn't until I was alone walking down the stairs that I remembered his wolf had promised mine the exact same thing.

It was laughable, really. What could Trace possibly know about the things I need?

Chapter 12

Trace had left me to my own devices with the explanation that he had a lot of work to catch up on. His being away for a month had left many of his alpha responsibilities unmet. I resisted the urge to remind him that no one had asked him to take that month off searching for me. There was no point in stirring the pot with him again, but it was exhausting having to bite my tongue and simultaneously fight against the desire to climb up on his body. Time away from him would be a welcome relief.

Besides, maybe now I could explore the house without Randy holding me back. Maybe I'd even be able to scope out a means of escape, though that idea had my wolf huffing again.

Downstairs, Justine was curled up in a blanket with a book and a cup of tea. I entered the expansive living room to join her, and I was instantly drawn to the oversized windows that had caught my eye the night before.

The view of Tumblewild's land from that spot was breathtaking. It showcased acres of hills and trees for as far as I could see. Occasionally, the rooftop of another home was visible in the distance, but other than that, it made me feel like I was standing on top of a secluded mountain. When I stepped away from the glass, I could see that Justine had been watching me with a slight smile on her face. Like her brother, she seemed to be much more subdued this morning.

"That view is one of the best parts of living in the alpha's house," she said, taking a sip from her mug. "Growing up, I always took it for granted, but this has become my favorite room for that very reason."

She patted the spot next to her on the deep leather couch, and I sat to join her. Her eyes swept over me, and she paused to focus on my turtleneck. She raised her eyebrows but didn't ask what might be hiding under the high collar. I looked away. The last thing I wanted to do was discuss that with her.

'So, Randy told me that you have been teaching at the school in town," she said instead, catching on to my discomfort. "Do you think you want to continue working there? Or are you going to take some time off?"

My look of surprise must have given her the wrong idea because she rushed to qualify her question. "Of course, as the alpha's mate, you don't have to work outside of the home. You can just help with pack business if you want instead. And I don't mean *just help with the pack* like that or anything. It will take a lot of time and effort to--"

"It's fine, Justine," I interrupted, saving us both from her rambling. "I'd love to continue working at the school. As an assistant, actually, not as a teacher. But I assumed that Trace wouldn't allow me to work there. Gabe and Randy didn't seem to think so, either."

Justine snorted. "He will absolutely allow it. It's helpful

to the pack and something for you to do so you don't drop dead from boredom," she insisted. "Don't worry; I'll talk to him about it."

I nodded, not wanting to argue. If she could get Trace to allow me outside of these walls, I wasn't going to second-guess her ever again. "So…you know Trace really well. Is there anything I should know about him? Besides to try and stay out of his way, I mean."

Justine tilted her head to the side and regarded me with interest. "Why do you think you need to stay out of his way? If I know my brother at all, he's going to want to see you all hours of the day."

I couldn't tell if she meant that as an innuendo, but I quickly prayed that no one else in the house knew about me sharing Trace's bedroom last night. "We just don't get along very well, and I think arguing is stressful for both of us. So, I'm going to try and stay out of his way as much as I can."

"What kinds of things do you argue about, though?" she pressed. "I don't doubt that you have argued a lot while he is trying to convince you to be his mate. He's stubborn, that's for sure. And last night really shouldn't count because he is kind of unstable at the moment, but if you give him a chance, I promise that he's actually one of the most level-headed guys I've ever met. Gabriel not included, of course. As an omega, Gabe's naturally more laid back."

My former roommate had struck me as an omega with how helpful and accommodating he was, but omegas in Dark Claw weren't allowed to be part of the pack council. I liked that Tumblewild didn't restrict positions on the council only to betas and other loud males.

There was something else that I wanted to ask, but it felt

weird to say it to Trace's sister. She saw my hesitation and motioned with her hand that I should just spit it out.

"Okay, you don't have to answer this if it's too weird...but Trace said something to me, and his wolf said the same thing to my wolf. I just wanted to know if you might know what he meant...."

"Maybe," she answered curiously. "What did he say?"

"He said that he would provide everything I need. Is that him saying that he will support me financially? Or emotionally?"

For the first time since I arrived, Justine blushed. "It's actually a promise that a lot of male werewolves make to their mates. Your mom never discussed this with you?"

I shook my head. "No, she died when I was young. My dad was her true mate, and after she passed on, he was...a little out of it. He wasn't himself without her, and eventually, we lost him, too."

Justine nodded, her eyes filled with sympathy. "Our parents are gone, too, but they died more recently. We had them with us until we were both adults, at least."

She paused and seemed to search for the right words. "When Trace said that to you, he was promising to give you the structure and discipline you need. Although, as your mate, he will provide those other basic things, too, of course. All male werewolves feel the need to take care of their mates. It's in their DNA or something. Alphas have a more stressful job because he also provides structure and discipline to the whole pack...but for you, it will be...different."

Justine's whole face was a deep blush at this point, and she was looking down at her mug to avoid my eyes. I felt bad for her but couldn't understand why she was so embarrassed. I could remember my mom having rules from my dad when she was alive but was that really something to blush over?

"Oh. Well, I guess I should tell Trace that I really don't need any of that, and he can save it for other members of his pack," I said. "My former alpha tried to give me discipline and structure a few times, and it never went over well."

She found my offer hilarious, and it seemed to help her get over her embarrassment. She laughed deeply, eyes sparkling.

"That's an entirely different type of thing, Mariam. Male werewolves are pretty much designed to dominate their mates, whether they're an alpha or not. The direction he gives to the rest of us is on an as-needed basis...and I can guarantee you that it's a different brand than what you'll receive," she said.

Her smile slowly disappeared, and she gave me a thoughtful look. "You are really independent and smart, which is great for our pack and for Trace, whether he wants to believe it or not."

I shrugged. "It just seems like another thing for us to argue about, to be honest. Dealing with someone who is as cranky as Trace day in and day out doesn't sound like fun at all." I paused, realizing that I was insulting her brother. "I mean, I'm sure that he's a great alpha and brother--"

"No, I get it. Trace has been a lot lately, and not in a good way. But I think you might underestimate him as a mate. He might surprise you. The goddess put you together for a reason, after all."

"Yeah, maybe." I suppressed the compulsion to roll my

eyes. As nice as Justine was, she just wouldn't be able to understand. Her relationship with Randy seemed…interesting…but they were also obviously happy together. She wouldn't know what it felt like to be tied to someone you didn't even want to be around.

A knock at the front door interrupted us, causing Justine to look over my shoulder. I knew Randy must be in view because her gaze softened, and she winked at him. The beta opened the door and greeted whoever was waiting.

"Hi, Randy. I heard that our alpha has returned, and I wanted to drop these off for him," a female voice answered as she crossed the threshold.

My wolf perked up, very aware that she sounded young and a little too excited about our mate returning to the pack. *Down girl,* I warned her.

Justine stood to greet the woman, and I followed, not wanting to be rude to the guest. She led me to Randy and a young brunette werewolf. She had dimples on both cheeks as she smiled at us.

"It's good to see you, Jess," Justine said as we entered the foyer. "This is Mariam. She's Trace's true mate."

Justine's introduction caused the other woman- Jess- to freeze and her smile to falter. The glimmer in her eyes dimmed a little, and it was clear she was struggling to hide her emotions. I frowned, knowing that her negative feelings must be directly tied to meeting me. I held out my hand to her.

"Hi, Jess. It's good to meet you."

She hesitated, but only for a fraction of a second before taking my hand and giving it a soft shake. Her sadness was morphing into worry and fear. I shot Justine a questioning look, but she was focused on the basket of muffins Jess was carrying.

"Are you Trace's friend?" I asked the woman. My wolf grumbled at the idea, but she was also aware of how intimidated the other wolf was of us already. This person wasn't a threat to our relationship with Trace, so thankfully, she stayed in check and didn't lash out at her. Jess's cheeks turned bright pink at the question.

"We were- I mean, I guess we are. But that was before, of course. Before he met you—"

Her rambling would have gone on for much longer, but Justine cut her off. "I'll take those muffins and give them to Trace for you," she said, easing the basket out of Jess's hands. Jess nodded, relief flooding her features.

"Thanks, Justine. I'll go and leave you all to it. Please tell Trace…er, I hope you all enjoy the muffins, that is."

Jess backed out the door and shut it behind her, leaving the three of us in the foyer. Justine and Randy each grabbed a muffin, but I just stared at the closed door.

"Who was that?" I asked.

Justine gave me a look of pity. "That's Jess. She's had a major crush on Trace for years. Like, since we were in elementary school together. She's always hoped that one day he would realize they were true mates."

"Or just give up on finding a true mate and be with her anyway," Randy added with a mouth full of muffin. "It's not a big deal, troublemaker. She's not as jealous of Trace as you are of me, obviously."

Justine scowled at him, but I was still focused on the girl who brought the muffins.

"Oh." What else could I say? Jess seemed really sweet and

was obviously afraid of my reaction to her being in love with Trace. My wolf already knew she wasn't a threat; the conversation we were having now wasn't even piquing her interest.

"Don't worry," Justine said, carrying the basket into the kitchen. "She was obsessed with him, but she won't do anything now that you're here. She just needs time to sort out her feelings."

I nodded, unsure if I should follow her or go back into the living room. What was I even supposed to do today? It was still only mid-morning, and soon, the kindergarten classes would be getting ready for their first recess. Maybe I should try to go to work.

Randy raised his eyebrows when I turned to him, almost as if he was reading my mind. "If you want to leave the house, you'll have to ask Trace."

I scowled at him. Being a prisoner wasn't appealing in the first place, and hearing something like that made my blood boil. But what could I do? No one was going to come and save me. *Unless Patrick makes good on his promise.*

The idea fluttered across my mind, causing my wolf to stir and glare at me. She wasn't a fan of that line of thinking, but him breaking me out of here might be my only hope, even if it was a long shot.

I begrudgingly walked with Randy into the kitchen. Justine was savoring the last of her muffin. Her mate reached for a second one, having finished his in a few bites. I sat on a barstool and watched as Justine pretended to swat his hand away before handpicking him one with extra berries in it. Randy gave her a warm smile when he bit into the dessert.

This quiet exchange was sweet and felt almost too intimate to watch. Obviously, Trace had seen them together. Did he think that we would be like that one day?

"What are your plans for today, Mariam?" Justine asked, interrupting my thoughts.

"I don't know what I'm allowed to do," I answered carefully, shifting my eyes to Randy. Justine scowled at that answer.

"Well, that's just ridiculous. Give me your phone, wolfman. I'm calling Trace," she demanded, hand outstretched to her mate. Randy sighed and handed his phone to her, grumbling under his breath about staying out of Trace's business. She dialed and held the phone up to her ear, giving me an apologetic look.

"Are you rude or just stupid?" Justine said when Trace picked up. My breath caught in my chest, worrying about how the moody alpha on the other end would respond. I had to remind myself that he probably wouldn't murder his own sister at least.

"You heard me," she said, walking to the fridge and fishing out a jug of milk. "You left a perfectly good mate here alone on her first day in a new pack, she doesn't know anyone, and your old flame Jessica just dropped off muffins for you. Fucking *muffins*, Trace. I tried to comfort Mariam and ask her out to do something, and do you know what she told me? "Justine paused for dramatic effect. "She said she didn't know what she was allowed to do. You have abandoned her, and she doesn't even know if she can leave the house."

Randy reached over and slapped her on the ass, growling a warning. Whatever the line was with them, Justine was getting close to crossing it. But while she was exaggerating about my reaction to Jessica stopping by and about this being my first day with the pack, I was also thrilled to hear her chewing Trace out. He needed someone to challenge him on his bullshit, and as much as I wished I could, the man was terrifying to me. Avoidance was a much safer route to take with him.

I expected to hear shouting through the other side of the phone, but instead, his voice remained soft enough that I couldn't even make out his response. Whatever he said, it must have been what Justine was hoping for. She gave me a bright smile and a thumbs up.

"See, was that so hard?" she asked. Justine didn't wait for her brother's answer. She ended the call and handed the phone back to Randy. Then she poured her mate a tall glass of milk, which seemed to help soothe his irritation at her behavior.

"Trace says you're free to leave the house," she said, putting the milk back in the fridge. "I can't wait to show you Flagstaff and introduce you to some other pack members. It's perfect timing, too. What with the pack run tonight and all."

My throat tightened. How could I forget about the pack run? I had been so excited about the possibility of joining Gabe and some of the women at work for the run, but now I wouldn't just be Ella...I wouldn't even be Ella at all, actually. I would be introduced as a liar and their alpha's runaway mate. My head started to spin as I thought about their reaction to learning that I had lied to them about my identity the whole time.

"Whoa," Randy said, reaching out to steady me. "Pack

runs are fun. It's nothing to be worried about. Didn't you have them in your former pack?"

I nodded, trying to suppress my uneasiness. I wanted to explain that they were actually one of the things that I missed the most about being away from my pack, but then another emotion rushed through me. This would be the first pack run where I didn't have Patrick and Lance running beside me.

"Do you want to go out today, or do you just need some time to rest?" Justine asked, watching me with a frown. "And if you aren't up to going on the run, I'm sure Trace would understand you sitting this one out."

I shrugged as I slid off the stool. I wanted to run back up the stairs and hide under the blankets on my bed. Maybe I could call Patrick again, though that made me feel inexplicably guilty. I made some lame excuse about needing to rest more before leaving the house and trudged back up the stairs.

I didn't want to go on the run, that much was for sure, and now I didn't even want to face the teachers at the school. I chastised myself for trying to avoid the inevitable. *When had I become such a coward?*

Running away was all I had done for the past month, and it seemed like I was making it a habit. Maybe it would be better to go and just face the music sooner rather than later. Unless I really could escape, I'd have to see them all again, anyway.

I fell facedown back onto the guest room bed. Slowly, I reached for the phone I had left abandoned on the floor and scrolled through the short list of contacts—Patrick, Ella, a few teachers from the school, the principal...and Gabe. I clicked on his name before I could second-guess myself and tentatively held the phone up to my ear.

For a minute, I thought he wasn't going to answer, but then he picked up right before it went to his voicemail. "Hey, Mariam. How's it going?"

It felt weird to hear him use my real name instead of calling me Ella, but I pushed the thought aside.

"It's okay. I guess…I mean, it could be worse." I tried to laugh, but it sounded forced. Gabe was quiet on the other end, waiting for me to elaborate. "I don't know what I'm going to do, Gabe. I just…I need a friend."

"Well, we're friends. What do you need me to do for you?" The question was measured. He was choosing his words carefully.

"I'm not asking you to break me out of here," I said, sighing. "I'm just really overwhelmed. I was thinking about the pack run tonight and facing everyone from school…and I think I'm losing my nerve. I just want to hide in this room forever."

"Well, you don't have to worry about the people at school. I called and let Ms. Jenkins know what was going on. I assumed that you wouldn't be in, at least today, and I didn't want them to worry." He paused. "She wasn't upset, Mariam. She was grateful that you were able to help when you could, and she wanted me to tell you to be kind to yourself if I spoke with you."

That made me feel pretty stupid. Of course, Ms. Jenkins would be more concerned about me than about who would cover for kindergarten. I was still a little surprised that she wasn't angry over being lied to, but maybe she understood more than I gave her credit for.

"Trace bit me this morning," I whispered into the phone. It still felt surreal to say the words out loud.

Gabe sucked in a breath. "And how do you feel about that?"

"I'm upset. My wolf is over the moon," I answered truthfully. "It's going to prevent me from ever leaving, isn't it?"

There was no point in lying to Gabe about my desire to escape. He wasn't going to betray me. At least, I didn't think he would report our conversation back to Trace.

"I think you should give him a chance," Gabe answered slowly. "But if you are still unhappy about being mated after really trying to be with him, we'll figure something out together, Mariam. I haven't spent hours in the Collections room at the library for nothing."

If there were any way out, he would be able to find it. "Gabe, I can never repay you for offering that. Thank you," I said, my voice cracking with emotion.

"I meant it when I said we are friends, Mariam," he replied. "But I also meant what I said about giving Trace a chance. The moon goddess has more insight than any of us, and don't toss away a chance at real happiness with a true mate over something stupid like pride."

I frowned. I was about to ask what Gabe meant by the cryptic warning, but he had to go. I hung up feeling much better about the day and my future and only a little guilty. I shoved the negative emotion down deep and got ready to leave the house with Justine.

Chapter 13

Before allowing us to leave, Randy had given Justine and me a long lecture about staying with the guards at all times, causing his mate to roll her eyes and me to agree readily to whatever terms he was offering. After my conversation with Gabe, I was itching to leave Trace's house and enjoy the day. Although, I did understand Justine's attitude, too. Having three male werewolves following us from shop to shop in Flagstaff felt excessive.

Randy clearly wasn't willing to take any chances with me escaping. He was needed for a few council meetings ahead of the pack run, so he assigned three of his best men to the job instead. Two of them seemed all business and a little upset when they met me. No doubt, they were recently returned pack members who had taken part of the "wild goose chase" to bring me here, as Randy had so eloquently put it.

The third one was younger, and he seemed excited to be part of the assignment. He joked around with Justine for most of the drive into the nearby city while I looked out the window and soaked up the Northern Arizona beauty.

My wolf wasn't interested in shopping or having lunch in

the city, but she did enjoy the scenery, too. We watched the landscape pass in comfortable silence. I could feel her excitement about the pack run without her saying a word. I hadn't let her out to run in over a week, so there was no way I would be able to deny her the chance to run with the others. We would be there, no matter how awkward it was.

"What made you change your mind about going out today?" Justine whispered.

She might as well have just said it in a normal voice, what with werewolf hearing. But then again, we were in the third row of the SUV, and the men in the front seemed more interested in the radio than our discussion. The young guy in the center had turned to talk with them, too, and something told me Justine wouldn't ask the question unless it was safe for me to answer.

"I talked to Gabe, and he made me feel a little better about everything," I said hesitantly. Justine's eyes widened a little bit at my admission.

"I wouldn't say that to Trace," she warned.

I gave her a look that told her I wasn't that much of an idiot, and she giggled in response. Of course, I left out the part about Gabe offering to help me find a way out of the mating bond. As cool as Justine was, she was still Trace's sister. Obviously, she would tell him something like that.

The driver spotted a parking space along the busy street and eased the large SUV against the curb. The younger wolf, whose name I learned was Jared, helped us out of the backseat, careful to only touch our hands. Justine reached up and pinched his cheek in thanks, causing him to blush.

"Let's start with lunch," she announced, gesturing to a restaurant on the corner. It was much larger than the small

Tumblewild diner. My stomach clenched and felt horribly empty as we reached the entrance and the wonderful smells met my nose on the sidewalk.

"See, I told you this wasn't the worst assignment ever," one of the tall bodyguards said, elbowing his friend.

"Wait until I tell Randy you said that, Craig," Justine threatened. She grinned as the werewolf's face paled. He opened the door for us, which earned him a smile from her.

I was about to follow her inside when my wolf perked up. She had caught a familiar scent, and her focus forced me to pause. I looked around, confused by her interest. Then, I spotted a young woman down the street.

Jess reddened and looked away when our eyes met. She had been watching us from a short distance, probably since we had left the car. Happy to find the source of the scent, my wolf shook and fell back on her haunches.

I hesitated only for a split second. I left the doorway and walked toward her. One of the men hurried to follow me, likely worried that this was some ridiculous escape attempt. I had the same thought- that Jess would take off as I closed the distance between us. But she remained, almost frozen in place.

"Hey, Jess," I greeted her softly. She gave me a cautious smile in return. She fiddled with the zipper on her jacket, betraying her nervousness. "Justine wanted to show me around Flagstaff, and we were just about to have lunch. Do you want to join us?"

My offer surprised us both. I wasn't usually a person who went out on a limb to make new friends, and she clearly thought I was harboring some kind of grudge. It looked like she would refuse, so I reached out and touched her arm.

"Look, I know that you and Trace had a close… friendship, and that isn't a big deal to me. Really. You guys can even continue being really good friends if you want."

Jess's eyes widened at my words, but her shock quickly morphed into confusion.

My wolf growled a warning to me, not supporting my offer at all, but I chose to ignore her. I wanted my freedom when it came to choosing friends, and that would never happen if I tried to gatekeep Trace's friendships.

"Why would you allow us to do that?" she asked.

I shrugged. "I don't own him."

The look on her face told me she thought I was nuts, but it didn't matter because she agreed to join us for lunch. As we walked back to the others, a new idea began formulating in my mind.

Jess became more comfortable with me as the afternoon passed. Justine raised a quizzical eyebrow at me when we walked up to the restaurant together. I could almost see the wheels turning in her head as she tried to figure out what game I was playing by inviting Jess to our afternoon out.

I smiled at her like I had no idea that befriending my mate's former flame was weird at all.

The sky started to darken, signaling that it was time to leave Flagstaff and head back to Tumblewild. The pack run was only a few hours off, and I shared my wolf's shiver of excitement. After making a few friends, I felt much more comfortable with the idea of running with the pack.

The ride back to pack lands was more subdued. Jess had driven herself, so it was only Justine and me in the backseat again. The younger male wolf -Jared- snored softly on the middle seat while the older two chatted in the front, once again oblivious to us. But unlike the ride that morning, Justine was lost in her own thoughts. I felt myself doze off as the swaying of the SUV lulled me to sleep.

"Everyone out," one of the male werewolves barked.

I started awake at the loud sound. We were back at the alpha house, and the moon was high in the sky, providing the only light other than the artificial lamps scattered across the vast property.

Justine moved around me and ducked out of the door without saying anything. I frowned, worried that my only friend in the alpha house was upset with me. I followed her, turning to climb out of the lifted SUV.

When I landed, my back met the hard chest of a male wolf. I spun around fast and found myself in Trace's arms. His strong hands settled on my ass, and he gave a satisfied grin. My heart raced, blood pumping in overtime at his touch.

I rose on my toes to crush my mouth against his. My hands buried themselves in his hair. His tongue licked the seam of my mouth, and I opened for him, eager for the intrusion. He devoured me like he was starving. I rubbed against his hard length that jutted against my stomach. Frustration coursed through me. Our height differences meant that I couldn't line him up against my core to get some relief.

He reeled back and grabbed the sides of my head to keep me from pulling him in for another kiss. "Hello, little wolf," he said, breathless. "Did you have a good time in Flagstaff?"

I nodded, my mind clearing just enough to process his question. He was so intoxicating. His smell and the hardness of his chest against my breasts drew me in again. My wolf shone through my eyes, eager to take our make-out session to the next level.

His wolf flashed briefly, but he blinked slowly and fought back control. "It's almost time for the pack run, little wolf. But don't worry; we'll finish this later."

His smirk brought me back to reality, and I scowled. I hated that he could get me going so easily. He wasn't even trying, and I had been this close to fucking him on the front lawn.

I untangled myself from his arms and pulled my shirt back down to cover my stomach. It had ridden up dangerously high, almost exposing the bottom part of my bra. I was thankful that the others had already dispersed and that the moon wasn't bright enough to see anything a few feet away. Undoubtedly, Trace was even more grateful. Male werewolves were known to start fights if their mate became exposed to someone else, particularly other males.

"Is there anything I need to do to prepare for the pack run?' I asked, slipping out of my shoes at the door. Trace's expression transformed to one of appreciation.

"Thank you for asking, but not this time. In the future, as the female alpha of the pack, you will be expected to help with preparations, but for now, all you need to do is show up and enjoy." He rose his eyebrows suggestively. "I am looking forward to admiring your beautiful wolf when I see her again, mate."

I didn't respond to him. At least, not verbally. I couldn't do anything to prevent the way my hormones reacted. There was a clear view of the bonfire and barbecue being set up in the backyard from the living room window.

Justine was already down there, along with Randy and the wolves who escorted us to Flagstaff. A few others that I didn't recognize stoked the flames as the smoke billowed high into the clouds.

"It's time for us to join them, Mariam," the alpha purred in my ear. I sighed and moved away from the window, indicating that he should lead the way.

He chuckled and took my hand. The warmth of this touch thrilled my wolf. She paused restlessly with anticipation, eager to be given control of our body. I didn't bother trying to calm her down. Soon, she would have what she wanted.

By the time we walked the long, winding path to the bonfire, a few thousand other wolves had gathered. Some had already shifted, while others struggled to keep their animal inside. A hush fell over the crowd as Trace and I joined them. All eyes were on him, though a few flickered between the two of us.

The combination of new and familiar werewolf scents assaulted my nose, but my wolf helped me separate the known and the unknown. Somewhere in the crowd, I could make out a few of the teachers from the school, Gabe, and Linda from town hall. Within eyesight, I could see Randy, Justine, and Jess.

"Thank you for joining us tonight," Trace said, addressing the entire group of werewolves. "I apologize for my absence from our pack lands, and I am happy to finally be home. Before we begin our run, I want to introduce you to my mate. Please greet Mariam Hinder, soon to be Mariam Everett."

The wolves who had already shifted howled while those in human form clapped and cheered. I raised my eyebrows at Trace; we had never discussed me taking his last name, but of course, he assumed that I would. He dipped down quickly to pull me into a chaste kiss. The surprise from the contact stole away my resolve and gave my wolf the opportunity she had been waiting for.

She forced the shift, shredding my clothes as our bones reset. She turned in a circle, showing off her beautiful coat to the audience and our mate.

Taking her cue, the remaining humans shifted and joined in her excitement. Trace was soon to follow. His wolf eyes sparkled, and he nuzzled against my wolf's neck. Throwing his head back, he howled to signal the beginning of the run.

It started slow, with the wolves in the back moving first, but soon everyone in the pack was pushing further into the trees. My wolf raced, waiting until the last moment to dodge the trunk of one tree and the low-hanging branches of another.

Trace snapped at my heels, warning me to be careful, but my wolf felt untouchable. Instead of cowering in obedience, she pushed herself to be faster and more agile. Too many moons trapped inside our human form had left her intoxicated on a werewolf high.

The alpha snarled at our insolence. The wolves around us slowed, not wanting to upset their leader, but my wolf darted away, leaving him in the dust. She joined another crowd within the pack, one that smelled of Gabe.

She found him quickly among the others and yipped with joy at their reunion. Gabe's wolf threw her a grin and moved faster to match her pace. Together they pushed themselves, breaking away from the herd. In her delirium, my wolf didn't see Trace coming up between them, moving to swiftly cut off her path and force her to change directions.

I felt my annoyance rise, but my wolf didn't experience

any of that emotion. She was excited to be running beside our mate again and wasn't concerned that he had prevented her from choosing her own way. Together, they led some wolves up the mountain and down again, creating a big loop around a natural pond. After a few hours, my wolf began to slow. Trace took notice and adjusted to keep in step with her.

She was hungry and getting tired. I wanted to kick myself with how out of shape she was. I should have committed to allowing her to shift and run at least once a week. Back home, we would just be catching a second wind. He shorted the run by herding my wolf toward the clearing. A few pack members had already shifted and were tending the food over the open flames. Wonderful smells filled the air.

Trace's wolf nudged me toward a set of tents. Obviously, they were there to be used as makeshift changing rooms, but my clothes had been destroyed during my sudden shift. Justine, already fully clothed herself, held open one of the doors for me. Inside, someone had brought down a sweatshirt and jeans from my room. I shifted quickly inside the tent, sighing with relief that my first time meeting the pack wouldn't include a naked walk of shame back to the alpha house.

I hurried to dress. The changing rooms often had a long line in the Dark Claw pack, and I didn't want to force others to wait. As I expected, a line had already formed when I exited the tent.

Despite feeling like a wimp, it seemed like most of the pack was either already back or was just arriving. Some wolves were actively changing into their clothes in the open, which wasn't unusual, either. Something told me that they were Tumblewild's single werewolves. Mated wolves had to deal with jealous partners who didn't appreciate others viewing intimate areas.

I scanned the crowd for Trace. My heart drummed in my chest when I found him leaning against a tree, chatting and laughing with Jess. My wolf was distracted, still riding the high from the run, but I could feel the mixed emotions just fine. I had told Jess I was okay with them being friends, so why did the scene unfolding before me hurt so much?

I swallowed the emotion, reminding myself of the plan I had hatched while in Flagstaff. I needed to talk with Jess again. She very well might be my ticket back home.

I slowly approached my mate, making sure to keep my eyes warm and unthreatened. I knew the moment he scented me because he straightened, trying to make the exchange between him and Jess look more transactional than friendly.

I wasn't fooled. They had been friends for years, and it was clear that they were both enjoying the conversation before I showed up.

Trace's eyes met mine when I gently touched his arm. He searched my face for signs of jealousy or anger. He seemed confused when there was no trace of those emotions on my features. He would have reacted completely differently if the situation had been reversed. Hell, all the mated werewolves I knew would, so his confusion was warranted.

"Hi, Jess," I said, smiling at her. She, too, looked worried about my reaction to the two of them laughing and talking alone. "It was nice spending the day with you in Flagstaff. We should hang out again soon."

She smiled and agreed, which caused Trace to narrow his

eyes. He could probably tell that I was up to something, but he couldn't work out what it was. I cleared my throat, thankful again that our connection wasn't complete.

"Are you free tomorrow? Do you want to come over for breakfast?" It felt odd to invite someone over to a house where I still felt like a visitor myself, but I needed to talk with her as soon as possible. And as long as I could keep my hands off the handsome alpha, I should still be able to prevent him from being able to access my thoughts by morning.

Her eyes flickered to Trace, asking for his permission without using words. He shrugged, still confused and more than a little wary.

"Sure," she said finally. "I'd love to."

Chapter 14

"I'm sleeping alone tonight, Trace," I said flatly. We were at a stand-off in the hallway, and he was blocking me from walking past his room. The alpha growled at my defiance, and it took all my resolve not to take the words back as soon as I uttered them.

The desire to submit to him was growing; I couldn't deny that anymore. But my need to put some distance between us was an even more pressing demand. I needed to have a clear, unreadable mind in the morning if I wanted any chance of succeeding, and if I was alone with him tonight, odds were good that we would end up consummating the relationship.

"You were the one who said we need to take this slow. You didn't want to pressure me into anything after biting my neck in a moment of weakness, remember?"

I felt like a heel throwing his words back at him. I had been so ready to fuck his brains out, and his ability to pump the breaks was the only reason I still had any agency at all. I should be thanking him for wanting to take it slow. Maybe one day I'd get the chance, but for now, I needed to focus all my energy on escaping.

Trace closed his eyes and considered my words. I didn't need telepathy to know he was arguing with his wolf. The creature wouldn't understand any reason to be apart from his mate. Taking things slow wasn't even a concept for him.

"I know that's what I said," he grumbled. "But that was when we were both too horny to keep our hands off each other. After the run, we should be able to control our wolves."

I snorted. "Yeah, great hold you have on him right now."

He sighed. "Fair point," he admitted. "He doesn't want to let you out of his sight, and neither do I. I don't know what you're up to, but I don't like it, Mariam. I'm not stupid enough to believe that you really want Jess to come to breakfast tomorrow, either, so don't even go there."

"Why wouldn't I want her over for breakfast? Aren't you just friends?" I asked as innocently as I could manage.

He scowled at me. "Of course, we're just friends. I would never betray you." His defensiveness quickly turned to curiosity. "But you don't seem jealous, and that is…odd."

"Why should I be jealous? You just said I have no reason to be." I shrugged, puzzling him even more.

"Of course, you have no reason to be. But…if you had been chatting with a male werewolf tonight, I would have reacted…differently. Any shifter would."

"Maybe we aren't true mates after all," I offered.

"No, you know better than that," he said, pulling me to him. He kissed the top of my head and tucked a stray curl behind my ear. Sighing again, he relented. "One night. You can sleep apart for one more night, since we didn't have much time to spend together today, but starting tomorrow, you are in our room every night. I'll cancel all my meetings if that's what it takes to make you more comfortable with our bond."

He released me before I could capture his lips with mine and stepped to the side to allow me to pass. As I walked by, his hand swiftly met my ass.

"Ow!" I said, jumping away.

"That's a reminder of what's to come, mate." Trace's voice was low and seductive, and I felt hot wetness pool in my underwear. His nostrils flared, scenting my reaction from several feet away. I turned and ran the rest of the way to my room, not trusting myself to stay with him any longer.

I propped the chair against the door and hurried to the bathroom, the only door in the bedroom with a lock. I clicked it in place and prayed that he wouldn't try to follow me. At least, the part of me thinking clearly hoped that he wouldn't. The other part of me wanted to leave and go to him myself.

It was confusing, to say the least. Whenever Patrick had tried to spank my ass, all I felt was pain and humiliation. But when Trace did it, it sent me into another world of horniness.

I rummaged through my things to find my shampoo and conditioner and then took a long, cold shower. I hoped the icy water would be enough to take my mind off Trace's firm hand on my behind, but it did nothing to help. I looked up at the pulsing shower head and bit my lip as a new possibility occurred to me.

Carefully, I removed the head from the harness and adjusted the temperature to a warm setting. I reached between my legs and gently separated my lower lips. I used my thumb to run the sensitive nub between the folds, causing pleasure to shoot through my body. I angled the water to first massage the passage of my vagina and then turned it upward to focus on the pulsing nerve.

Memories of the things Trace had shown me replayed in my mind, soon replaced by a scenario of my own. I saw his hard body forcing mine deeper into the mattress of his bed, and he held me there despite my screams of passion. I heard myself cry that it was too much, that he was too much, for me to take. That didn't stop him at all; the imaginary Trace continued to force his thick cock into my pussy. In and out, in and out, while he whispered what a dirty slut I was in my ear.

It didn't take long for me to climax. I bit my lip to avoid crying out as I found release. My legs felt like rubber as I turned up the pressure on the showerhead, forcing myself to experience wave after wave of pleasure. Finally, I couldn't take anymore and turned the water off.

I prayed and waited in the silence of the bathroom, hoping that my sounds of orgasm hadn't broadcasted to Trace down the hall.

He was upset the last time I attempted to masturbate, so a full session with a showerhead would likely rile him up even more. Plus, if he had any idea that my thoughts were of us, he would probably break down the door to make the fantasies a reality.

Several minutes passed without so much as a knock on the door, and I began to breathe easier. My wolf stretched, content that we were able to blow off some of the steam that had built inside of us.

I returned the shower's nozzle to its holder and laughed at how shaky my legs were trying to get out of the bathroom. It felt like ages since I had climaxed like that. And I never had from a solo session, that's for sure!

The following day, I woke up to pounding on the bedroom door. I stumbled to my feet and removed the chair wedged beneath the handle. "Who's there?" I called out.

"Who do you think?" Trace answered. I frowned at his moody response. Well, if he was going to be an asshole about it…

"You're going to have to tell me. Too many men are coming in and out for me to keep track." I grinned to myself, knowing that the response would get under his skin. I opened the door and faced my captor.

"Cute," Trace spat, pushing his way inside. "You know, the house is perfectly safe. You don't need to worry about someone breaking in." I raised an eyebrow at him, causing him to chuckle. "And if it's meant for me, then you'd need a lot more than that to stop me from getting inside." He pointed to the chair, and I sighed, knowing that he was right.

"Well, what's all the commotion about? It's only—" I paused to glance at the clock on the wall "—seven-thirty. Jess won't be here for another few hours."

"True, but I need to talk with you. I won't be here for breakfast. There's some pack business that must be dealt with, and I'll do my portion from the house. I should be done by around noon. I'm sending Randy and Justine out to take care of the rest on site."

"You don't trust me enough to leave me here while you go on a business trip," I said. It was more of a statement than a question. It was painfully apparent that he didn't trust me at all. And for good reason.

"Why did you invite Jess to breakfast today?" Trace shot back, changing the subject, and narrowing his eyes suspiciously. "I don't share her interest in pursuing anything more than a friendship, but I won't stand by if you're planning to treat her poorly. She had a childish crush long before I met you and...."

I held up my hand and rested it on his chest. Trace stilled at my touch, his voice faltering mid-sentence. "I'm not going to be mean or rude. She seems nice. That's all."

Well, that was a bald-faced lie. I was also hoping she would be game for trying to win Trace's affection, or at the very least, seducing him. Maybe if he got a taste of her, I would be off the hook. All it would take was a bite to her neck and a good fuck to guarantee my release.

My wolf snarled, threatening to shift and reveal the plan to Trace's animal. The words spoken between them had been few, but she already felt an unwavering loyalty toward him. I shut that shit down right away.

We're not shifting. I am doing this for our own good. Just settle down and let me take care of it, I warned. She glared back, letting me know that I was on thin ice with her. Hopefully, I'd be able to get through the discussion with Jess, and she'd be able to spend some time with Trace before my wolf put her foot down and fought me earnestly for control.

Trace still didn't look convinced, so I changed the subject. "After Jess leaves, can I go back to the school and work there until dismissal?"

He blinked and scowled. "You are an alpha in this pack, Mariam. There is no need for you to have a job outside of your service to the pack here. We might not be officially mated with a ceremony, but you are still my mate in the eyes of everyone who matters. And I plan to rectify those other details as soon as I can."

He reached out to pull me to him, but I stepped away. I wouldn't have had the fortitude to resist his embrace yesterday. It was becoming easier to reject him and his charm the longer we put off completing the mating ritual. Trace had caught on to that fact, as well.

He growled low as he pursued me. I continued moving away until my back was against the wall, and there was nowhere else to go. His strong arms boxed me in, trapping me on both sides. I felt my eyes turn feral; even I wasn't immune to something this sexy.

"I want to see you like this all the time, mate. I want you helpless to resist me," Trace rumbled in my ear. "As soon as I start fucking you, you won't be able to pull away like that ever again. You'll want to obey me. You'll offer me that sweet pussy anytime I need it."

I gulped, struggling in vain to even out my breathing. *Think,* I prodded myself. *What were you going to ask him? What were you even talking about?* Oh right…going to work at the school.

I forced my wolf back inside. I was determined to keep control over her, now more than ever. I licked my lips, preparing to talk more about work, but the movement drew his attention to my mouth, and that brought his wolf to the surface. That wasn't what I was trying to do at all.

"Little wolf, your human needs to understand our ways. I have claimed you with my bite, but I need you to be mine in every sense. Why does she fight my human on this matter?" The wolf's voice was a few octaves lower than even Trace's baritone speaking voice, once again causing me to lose my train of thought.

I fought my wolf as she struggled to answer him. If I let her to the surface now, there's no telling what she might say. Trace's wolf watched our inner battle with interest, his dark eyes piercing my soul as he searched for an explanation.

"I want my freedom," I spat out at him. That wasn't a lie, at least, and it seemed to provide the wolf with something to consider.

"You may think you want freedom, little wolf, but what I have planned for you is much more in line with your real needs. Soon, I will be your master, your owner, and I will consume your every thought. That might sound like bondage to you now, but it is our way. You will receive freedom in your connection to me."

Satisfied with his words, the wolf left Trace's eyes, but the intensity in them remained. Trace might not have spoken the words himself, but he fully endorsed the message. "What do you think of that, sweet Mariam? Are you ready to become mine?"

Not waiting for a response, he thrust his hips against mine, bending his knees so that we lined up perfectly. His cock was hard, almost like steel, through his pants. It was long and thick; I could feel it clearly even with our clothes acting as a barrier.

His hands tangled in my hair until one of them found my throat. I melted against his grasp, once again surprised by how wonderful it felt. He applied light pressure, just enough to remind me that his strong fingers were allowing me to take each breath.

He moved his lips from my mouth and made a trail of kisses down my face. He nipped at my neck, grazing the fully healed scar he had left the day before. Just him lightly stimulating the mating mark sent me crashing into an orgasm. I screamed his name as I shuddered against him.

"Fuck, Mariam," he groaned. "You're going to make me lose control. If you don't want this…if you want to wait…please tell me. I'll stop. I promised you that I would, and I'll stop now if you want."

The desperation in Trace's voice made me want to undress him even more, but his plea reminded me of what I needed to do. It took every ounce of resolve left in my body to speak the magic words.

"I want you to stop," I whispered. He stepped back without complaint, but his eyes told me that it was incredibly difficult for him to do so. The air between us felt cold with his warmth gone.

I hurried out the bedroom door, not daring to stay in the room a minute longer. I needed to talk to Jess before things got out of hand, and I lost my freedom to a man like Trace Everett.

The phone was really nice, much fancier than the one I had left back at Dark Claw. I was alone in the kitchen admiring the gadget that one of Trace's men had shoved in my hands. He had left without any explanation, so my best guess was that Trace wanted me to start using it.

The kitchen was eerily quiet after he was gone. Justine and Randy would be absent most of the day, completing whatever business Trace had delegated to them. As far as I could tell, they were the only other people living in the expansive home, and they didn't even reside the main house, either.

According to Trace, the beta suite on the bottom floor was basically a separate apartment. I wouldn't even necessarily know when they returned if they used their private entrance.

I sipped the coffee I had brewed and flipped another pancake on the griddle. I had promised Jess breakfast, and coffee and pancakes were almost foolproof. I considered trying to find Trace and offer him a plate, but I thought better of it. We both needed space after what happened in the bedroom.

There was a tentative knock on the door right at nine-thirty. Of course, Jess would be on time. I got the impression that she was usually a rule follower, which would be an excellent fit for someone like Trace. He'd have her submitting to his kinky fantasies in no time.

I set down the spatula and hurried to the door, not wanting to argue with my wolf about another woman receiving Trace's kinks. She was an eager participant if there ever was one. In fact, she didn't even see what was so taboo about it; his interest in us was just par for the course in her mind.

"Good morning, Jess," I said, opening the door and welcoming her inside. She smiled and removed her coat before following me into the kitchen. "Your muffins were so good. I hope you don't mind having regular pancakes from a box mix. I'm not a talented chef."

Jess giggled. "It really wasn't anything. I'm sure these pancakes are delicious. Thanks again for inviting me over."

The laugh lines around her eyes told me that she genuinely appreciated the offer, but she was also discreetly scanning the room.

"Trace is somewhere in the house, but I don't think he'll be joining us for breakfast," I said.

Jess nodded and managed only to look slightly disappointed. She sat down on a barstool and returned her attention to me as I handed her a mug of coffee and some creamer.

"I'm grateful for the invitation to see you again, Mariam," she said carefully. "But I have the feeling that this is more than just a social call. Is there something you wanted to discuss with me? Away from Trace?"

She was clever; I had to give her that.

I nodded. "I wanted to share an idea with you. But before I do, I have to warn you that what I'm going to say is pretty unconventional, and I understand if you don't want to do it. I don't want to ruin your friendship with Trace, but I think you might like what I have to say."

Jess straightened in her chair, her interest piqued. I took a deep breath and continued. I explained to her how I wanted her to seduce my mate, convince him to mark and sleep with her, and break the bond we had with each other.

She listened without saying a word, mulling over the request in silence. When I finished, she took a long drink from her mug. I thought for sure she was going to refuse to help me, but she surprised me when she finally set her coffee back down on the counter.

"I'm in," she said.

Chapter 15

Jess and I discussed the details of how to pull off my idea over breakfast. She knew Trace well enough, but I offered a different perspective and some ideas of what might drive him wild.

"Submit to him, but not right away. I get the feeling that he likes a little bit of a fight," I said. "He seems to thrive on a power struggle to a point."

She nodded, taking mental notes with a blush on her cheeks. No doubt, she was a virgin, and this was new territory for her.

While being with Trace had conjured up some unique desires in me, the things he enjoyed weren't too different from some of the shit Patrick and Lance tried to talk me into. I smiled, remembering Lance's excitement when I agreed to light bondage during sex one night. I had to admit that I enjoyed it, too.

"What if he still isn't interested, even if I put all this out there?" Jess's voice broke a little. She seemed self-conscious, just imagining being turned down by her alpha. It must have been heartbreaking for her the first time it happened. Being half-dressed and vulnerable would no doubt make his rejection much more painful if it occurred again.

I reached over and gave her a reassuring touch. "Trace has been really sexually frustrated. I don't think that's going to be a problem at all. Besides, you're gorgeous, and you both have feelings for each other already."

My wolf whined, not wanting to believe that our mate might enjoy the comforts of anyone besides us.

Well, if he does, maybe he isn't our true mate, I said to her. She considered my point, tilting her head in thought. Finally, she seemed to agree. For her, this would be a test of his worthiness for us. Though our reasoning was different, it felt good to finally agree with her over something. Arguing with the animal was exhausting.

"Can I ask why you don't want to be with Trace? I'm far from the only one interested in him in Tumblewild. Most women here would jump at the chance to have him for a mate," Jess asked, genuinely intrigued.

I sighed. "I don't doubt it. I think most she-wolves would love to have someone like Trace."

"Then why?" Her eyes widened slightly as a new idea occurred to her. "Do you have an interest in another man? Someone from your former pack?"

"Yep. That's it," I said, wanting to end the conversation. Trying to explain my motivations for not wanting to bond with him wouldn't do any good. It wouldn't have made any sense to her, anyway.

That explanation seemed to satisfy her and end the line of questioning. By the time Jess left the house, we had a firm plan in place for transferring Trace's affection to her. I walked her to the door, excited to put it into motion that evening.

I wrapped my arms around myself and wandered the main floor, once again all alone. I busied myself cleaning up the kitchen and scrubbing the griddle. When I was finished, I stood back and admired the gleaming countertops and stack of clean dishes. That had been my job back home with Ella; she cooked, and I cleaned in order to keep the house in working order.

The clock on the wall said it was already almost eleven. Trace had all but forbade me from going back to work at the school, and Gabe was undoubtedly busy working at town hall. I pulled the new smartphone from my pocket and scrolled through the contacts.

Trace had added himself, Randy, and Justine. There was also Jared and a few other men that were probably members of the babysitter's club that had taken us to Flagstaff. I hovered over Trace's name before pushing it. He answered right away.

"Mariam," he said. I couldn't help but frown at the way he said my name. It felt icy and formal.

"Trace," I answered. "Jess just left. I know you don't want me going to the school, but can you tell me what it is I can do while I'm here at the house?"

He paused, considering my request. "You can always come up and help me in the office."

"What do you need help with?" I asked, suspicious that he was really just looking to continue what we had started in the bedroom.

"Filing. Maybe making some calls for me. You know, personal assistant stuff," he said. "I had one, but she's out on maternity leave, so I've honestly been a little swamped."

My wolf bristled at the thought of Trace working with

another woman so closely, which almost made me laugh out loud. She was on board with helping Jess seduce our mate but him working with another woman in a professional capacity was crossing the line for her.

Trace must have anticipated her getting her back up, and I could feel his grin through the phone. "Tell your wolf that my assistant doesn't possess a fraction of your allure."

His words seemed to appease her, and she curled back up in the corner.

"I don't even know where your office is," I pointed out. The house had at least ten doors on the second floor alone. Trace gave me quick directions, and I soon found myself standing next to him in front of a leaning stack of papers.

"You need to give your assistant a raise," I said, eyeing the mess.

Trace barked a laugh and ran a finger down my back. "She is compensated well, but with you as an assistant, I might include a few special bonuses."

His lips found the sensitive spot on the back of my neck. He sucked there gently, sending shivers down my spine. I put up my hands to push him away, but he caught me by the wrist before I could touch him.

"I think it's time to start establishing some rules for you, mate," he said, giving me a light squeeze. His voice was serious, causing my pride to prickle.

"I'm fine, thanks."

"I say you need them, so you need them," Trace chuckled. He brought my wrist to his mouth for a kiss, creating new butterflies in my stomach. "The first rule is that you don't try to push me away. Ever. If my touch is too much or you need me to stop, you need to use your words, and I'll stop."

His promise made me suspicious until I remembered that morning when he had pulled away at my request. Maybe he would be able and willing to stop without me pushing him away. I nodded, causing him to grin broadly.

"Good girl," he purred. He kissed me on the forehead and turned to grab some file folders and labels. "I need you to sort through all this mess. Some of the papers are bills or invoices. They have all been paid, but we need to keep them for taxes. Others are minutes from council meetings, and then there are some things that might have to be labeled as 'miscellaneous.' Just do your best and use as many folders as you need. I have a conference call starting in a few minutes, but just send a text or come find me if you need me. I'll be in there."

He pointed to one of the interior doors within the wing. It had his name on it, which I suppose made sense. Two other doors were labeled for Randy and Justine. An unlabeled one next to his told me it was likely intended for the alpha's mate, but I didn't want to ask. Instead, I just nodded and returned my focus to the pile on the secretarial desk in the center of the open room.

An hour and a half passed, but finally, the papers were sorted, and the folders were full and labeled. I grabbed a drink from the water cooler and surveyed the difference, pleased with my work. A small voice inside hoped that Trace would be happy with it, too.

I walked to the door and paused before knocking. He was so quiet in his office that part of me wondered if there was another door in there that allowed him to leave undetected.

"Come in," he said. I turned the handle and smiled at the man behind the desk. His tie was undone, and his long hair was ruffled from running his hands through it. He had never looked sexier.

"The filing is done," I said. "Is there anything else you need me to do?"

The offer earned me a wolfy grin. "Feeling rather submissive today, are we, mate? You have no idea how much I like to hear you ask me questions like that."

I blinked. I was just trying to be helpful since I was living in the house, too. My behavior had nothing to do with any desire to submit to him. Although, I might not have asked the question if he hadn't looked so appealing when I walked in.

I shook the unwanted thought away and glared at him. "Should I take that to mean I'm free to go?"

"If you wish," Trace said. "I was just thinking of taking a break for lunch. Do you want to join me?"

All the fight left me at the mention of food. I sighed and nodded, much to his approval. He stood and grabbed his jacket from the back of his chair and extended his arm for me to hold. I rolled my eyes but found myself reaching for it anyway.

"Just wait until you're calling me 'sir.' Or better yet, 'master,'" he whispered, squeezing my hand. I pulled my arm back quickly and scowled. Like that would ever happen.

Watching Trace cook had been an unexpectedly good time. He had rolled up the sleeves on his white shirt and turned a list of simple ingredients into a delicious salmon and white rice meal. I hadn't expected the powerful wolf to know anything about seasoning fish or pairing it with wine, but by the time he finished, it was one of the best meals I had ever eaten.

His eyes had shifted momentarily when I groaned at the first bite. No doubt, the sound had inspired some carnal thoughts for him, and I smiled beside myself. It was good to know that I wasn't the only one to have an embarrassing moment or two of unexpected horniness. Hopefully, Jess would inspire the same kind of reaction during her visit to his room that night.

Once again, I was thankful that our connection wasn't complete. But something else was changing and binding us together. I frowned, starting to realize that Trace's jabs about my obedience and submission to him were rooted in fact. Disobeying was becoming more difficult. Maybe Gabe would have some idea of what I could do to curb the effect.

"What are you thinking about, little wolf?" Trace asked from the other side of the table. His question startled me. I fought the urge to answer truthfully, settling on vagueness instead.

"The future," I said honestly. "And the present."

He grunted a laugh. "Well, at least you're not focusing on the past, I guess."

"What are you thinking about?" I asked. It was polite to return the question, but I was also genuinely interested in the answer. *What occupied Trace's mind in between the intense emotions and horniness?* I wondered.

"I was thinking about Justine and Randy, hoping that they're almost done dealing with the alpha of Sweetwater," he said. "They are our neighbors to the south. Our relationship with them has been... strained lately."

I nodded, though I had not heard of the Sweetwater pack before. They must be small or new. "Do you think they won't be successful?"

"Not at all. They are the best ones to do it. The issue is over an alliance Sweetwater might make with Randy's former pack, and we want to make sure they know who they're making friends with. Once they hear what Randy and Justine have to say, my guess is that any chance of an alliance is over."

We finished the meal, and I got up to clear the dishes. Trace watched my every move but refrained from commenting. I knew he probably saw cleaning up after us as a submissive action toward him, and he could go ahead thinking that. My real goal was to get the mess cleaned up as soon as possible, so I could discuss the new developments in the mating process with Gabe.

At least, that's what I was telling myself. I didn't care one bit the way his eyes radiated with approval, and I certainly didn't walk with a sway to show off my ass when I knew he was looking.

Trace caught me by the hip and pulled me to him when I was done. I instinctually spread my legs so that I was straddling his lap. My mind buzzed as my sex made contact with his through our clothing.

"Do you know what it does to me to watch you clean up our mess?" he asked, flexing his hips to show me the result. I groaned aloud as the thick ridge in his pants pushed against my core. I rocked against it, not caring about anything other than creating some friction.

"Fuck, Mariam. If you keep doing that, I'm going to shoot my load in my pants like some teenager," he growled low.

"That would make us even," I said, remembering how hard I had come earlier that day in his arms. I reached down between us and stroked his engorged cock. By the time he cried out his release, my hands were wrapped firmly around him, pumping his shaft through the wool fabric of his pants.

He grabbed the back of my head, fisting my hair and forcing his mouth on mine while he rode out the orgasm. He bit down hard on my lip as I milked him and drained every last bit of cum from his dick. I tasted the blood as it filled my mouth, and the sweet pain was enough to send me over the edge with him.

———

"It's getting worse," I whispered into the cheap burner phone. "I don't know how much longer I can keep this up, Gabe. I don't want to be with Trace. I want to go home. But I'm starting to obey him…and it's getting hard not to just rip my own clothes off and jump on him. The horniness seemed to go away for a while, but now it's back. It's worse than ever. Why?"

To his credit, Gabe took the intimate details of my weakness in stride. I had the feeling that he really wanted to help me.

"From everything that I have read, that's part of the mating bond. Female werewolves experience waves of bonding emotions. After the initial bite, sexual tension begins for them until the act is complete. If they don't mate, for whatever reason, her body forces those feelings to become dormant, so she doesn't go crazy with lust, you know? Especially if the mating bite was given against her will."

I nodded. The attraction I had felt at first after the bite had been too intense to maintain with no relief. I was thankful the moon goddess provided me with that protection, at least.

"But dormant doesn't mean gone," Gabe continued. "That desire is still there, just below the surface. And when the next phase of bonding occurs for her, it is common for the desire to reignite."

"And the next phase of bonding is...what?" I asked though I was pretty sure that I knew what the answer would be.

"Submission," he answered. "Like the sexual attraction, it will ebb and flow for you as it continues to build. Female mates need to have the drive to submit for them to live harmoniously with their male counterparts. You probably felt the pull with Trace from the start, but now you're noticing it growing, right? His desire to master you and make you submit is increasing, too." He didn't wait for me to answer. Of course, I had already said as much. My instincts were working in overdrive. "If you stop fighting the urge, the desire to submit will lead you into giving him what he wants. Which right now, of course, is sex. He's as drawn to you as you are to him, though unfortunately for him, he gets no relief. His job is to push things forward and allowing him respite wouldn't be conducive with that."

I had to feel a little bad for Trace. He was constantly battling against his baser instincts to ensure that I was a willing, consenting participant. And so far, I had to admit that he was doing a pretty good job.

"I think I have a plan, a way to get out of this," I said,

making sure to keep my voice low. Trace had left the house for a run about ten minutes earlier. Getting him off had lightened his mood and earned me a bit of trust, it seemed. "Jess is going to come over tonight and try to seduce him in his bedroom."

Gabe groaned. "That's not going to end well, Mariam. And honestly, I'm surprised that you're willing to put Jessica through that. It's going to hurt her a lot when he rejects her again."

"She knows the risks," I said, frowning. "We discussed it this morning, and she understands that the mating bond might make it impossible for him to accept her. But it's worth a shot. If he gives in to her, they can be mated, and I can go home. Everyone wins."

"Is that really what you want?" Gabe asked. I furrowed my brow at the question.

"Of course. I want to be free," I said, exasperated by the question. I paused before continuing. "There is one more thing…if I can't resist Trace and he doesn't choose to be with Jess…he did something before, when we were connected in our dreams. He shut off the telepathy connection. Could I do that if the connection was complete, I mean?"

"Yes, there is a way," Gabe answered slowly. "Most mated couples find the missing connection too painful, but the goddess might have your back in that way, too."

I leaned in, eager to hear how to keep my thoughts safe from the man who wanted inside my head.

Chapter 16

The run was nice, but it paled in comparison to the feeling of Mariam's hands on Trace's body. Even now, he found himself savoring the way she had turned into a vixen, a total temptress when she straddled his lap and reached between them to fist his dick. He hadn't planned on doing anything other than just having lunch with her, but watching her complete tasks for him, first at his direction with the filing and then on her own with the dishes, had turned things inexplicably sexual. She had noticed Trace watching her, too. One day, he would have her clearing their table in the nude, giving him an unobstructed view of her perfect body as she served the alpha.

Trace adjusted himself, irritated that the thought was making his pants tight again. It wouldn't do any good to be rock hard when debriefing with Randy and Justine about their trip to Sweetwater. Thankfully, just the thought of talking with his sister was enough to take the wood out of his dick.

Although…maybe he could put it to good use with Mariam before the betas returned. The hope was enough to revive his cock almost instantly.

A part of him wondered if he had been too rough with her, though. Trace chastised himself as he remembered how he had pierced her lips with his canines. She had cried out--either in pleasure or pain, it was difficult to tell. The look in her eyes had told him she enjoyed it, but it was hard to know for sure without asking. He needed to have a conversation with her about that soon to prevent things from escalating things in the wrong direction physically if rough play wasn't appealing to her, but something told him that his sexy mate liked things a little kinky.

Trace slowed in front of the alpha house. The streetlights were already on, signaling that he should return home, if for no other reason than to sample more of his mate. Maybe soon, she'd be ready for everything their union could provide. His body hummed at the idea.

When he entered the front door, Trace couldn't help but picture what it would be like to have her waiting there to greet him, eager to serve him in every way. It would take time to train her. He needed to move slowly so she wouldn't fight so hard against being obedient. Though he had to admit— it was more than a little fun to play into the power struggle with her.

"Mariam," he called up the stairs, removing his earbuds. Trace frowned when she didn't answer. *Was it a mistake to leave her here alone? Had she run away?* Just the thought of having to track her down again made him see red. But no— her scent was still in the air. She was here, somewhere in the house. His eyes widened at another smell that settled in the air. *Was she wearing perfume?*

The alpha took the stairs two at a time, eager to find the woman who was attempting to seduce him. She didn't need perfume; her scent was intoxicating on its own, but the idea that she was doing it to draw him in had Trace chomping at the bit.

He frowned again when he caught a whiff of my own body odor. After the long run, Trace was more than overdue for a shower. He chewed on the inside of his cheek, trying to decide if he should forgo the shower and search for her or offer her a more appealing version of himself by cleaning up first.

He could wait a few minutes to shower, though his wolf told him he was making a mistake by not searching for her immediately.

Trace tossed his clothes in the hamper and made quick work of scrubbing himself down. He was going to grab a new outfit from the closet but thought better of it. Maybe Mariam would have a harder time resisting if he came to her in only a towel.

The alpha slung the oversized white towel low on his hips, leaving little to the imagination. If she came to him like that, he wouldn't have a chance in hell. Hopefully it would have the same effect on her. Trace combed his hair and pulled it back, grateful to get the wet mess out of his face. *There. That's as good as it's going to get,* he thought.

The smell of perfume intensified as he walked to the bathroom door, alerting him that Mariam must be on the other side.

He ran my finger over the edge of the towel, silently debating if he should remove it and greet her in the nude. Trace had no problem doing it, but she had only seen him completely naked once after a shift. Would it be crossing a line to surprise her like that?

He wasn't happy at the thought that she might not jump willingly into his arms, but he kept the towel firmly in place. Trace took a deep breath and opened the door leading to the bedroom.

His eyes landed on her legs first; they were bare, as was the rest of her save for a tiny pair of panties and a tight corset that caused her breasts to spill over the top. The primal beast in him loved the sight until his eyes traveled high enough to see her face. His wolf erupted, furious at the deception. It wasn't Mariam at all.

"What the fuck are you doing here, Jessica?" His anger caused her to cower in fear, but he was beyond caring. "What the fuck are you wearing? Fuck!"

Trace wanted to run back into the bathroom, but the alpha in him refused. A member of his pack had defied basic werewolf standards by showing up like this in a mated wolf's room. His animal pushed forward, wanting to deal with this on his own, but Trace fought back.

Jess started crying, fumbling to put on the robe she had discarded on the bed. He stood fuming, eyes averted. Trace wouldn't betray Mariam by looking at her again until she was properly covered. His wolf growled in agreement, glad that we were of one mind.

"I'm sorry, Trace," she choked out. "I know that you weren't interested before. But you have been under so much stress...and I thought that maybe you'd be open to—"

"Open to what, exactly?" he asked, interrupting her. "You're a sad replacement for my mate. We were friends as kids, and I thought we were friends as adults, too, but I am not going to put up with this, Jessica. You owe Mariam an apology for approaching me like this. She'll determine your fate. Let's go."

He grabbed her by the wrist and dragged her out of the bedroom. Having Jess in there, even with the robe tightly cinched around her waist, felt dirty. He thundered down the hallway until he reached Mariam's temporary sleeping space.

The handle wouldn't give when Trace tried to turn it. *Damn her and that fucking chair.* He wasn't going to let it stop him from getting to her; not now, not ever. He stepped back and kicked against the heavy wood, splintering it apart and tearing it off the hinges. Mariam scrambled to her feet, looking first at her mate and then at Jess next to him. Her face paled, and she looked like she might be sick.

Trace's heart did a double-take. In his haste, he had probably terrified her. She was a victim in this, too. He shoved Jessica to her knees at Mariam's feet.

"This pack member was in our room. I thought she was you until I saw her," he explained through gritted teeth. *How could I have been so stupid?* "The way I see it, she has offended you even more than me. As furious as I am, I leave her punishment in your hands, mate."

Mariam swallowed hard. Jessica was openly sobbing on the floor. She refused to look up and meet her alpha female's eyes. That sparked anger anew in Trace, and he grabbed her hair at the base of her head and jerked her face upward.

"You will look upon the woman you have wronged," he spat.

Mascara was running from her eyes in a way that he would have found appealing on Mariam, but on Jess, it struck him as just pathetic. His packmate, his friend, wasn't big enough to face her own fate. *How could I have been so wrong about her all this time?* he wondered. Trace had stood up for her, defended her, to Mariam, but in the end, she had betrayed his trust.

His eyes returned to his mate. He needed to convey his regret to her and apologize for his blindness, but something stopped him. Mariam wasn't angry. Instead, she looked worried. The blush that spread across her face reflected shame, but how could that be?

Gently, she reached down to pull Jess to her feet. She wiped the girl's tears away using the sleeve of her sweater and hugged her. Trace grit his teeth, the pieces slowly, too slowly, falling into place.

"You were behind this," he said, his blood boiling. "You sent her to my—our—room like a whore."

"I'm so sorry, Jessica," Mariam said, tears running down her face now, too. "Go home. You didn't do anything wrong. I'm so sorry."

Jess didn't have to be asked twice. She hurried to leave, refusing to meet Trace's eyes as she disappeared. Mariam and the alpha stood facing each other, neither of them saying anything until they heard the front door shut.

"Undress yourself and come to our room," he growled. Without waiting for an answer, Trace left Mariam to prepare herself. Not even she had the gall to ignore his command right now.

He went straight to work when he returned to the bedroom. Trace opened the chest at the foot of the bed and began selecting the device to use. Initially, he set out a cane and single tail whip, but after taking a deep breath, he changed his mind and returned them to the chest.

As much as he wanted to use them and cause Mariam

some real pain, this was probably her first time being disciplined by a partner. He would need to take it slow and build her up to receiving the heavier equipment. At least, that had been Randy's advice when he gifted Trace the kit during their search for his mate.

It was tradition, the best man gifting the tools of discipline when his friend took a mate. Trace was tempted to use them that first night he returned home to find Mariam living in Tumblewild, but her newness had stopped him. There was no getting out of this, though; she had earned this spanking, and he was the one to give it to her.

Trace gripped the handle of the widest paddle in the collection, knowing that the pain would be more evenly distributed across her whole ass by using it. It wouldn't be comfortable by any stretch of the imagination, but it would make it more manageable for her. He closed the chest and stood, waiting for his mate.

There was a gentle knock on the door before it opened a few inches, and Mariam shuffled in. She was glorious, completely nude, with her eyes averted. Blood rushed to his dick, and he removed the towel around his waist in one quick motion. She would see the effect that her punishment had on him, whether she wanted to or not.

Trace sat on the bed and patted his lap. "Sit," he commanded.

Mariam's eyes widened as she looked up to take in the sight of his fully engorged member. She didn't look scared, as a virgin might, but instead, she looked…hungry.

Her gaze lit a fire in Trace's chest, and he wanted nothing more than to grab her and throw her onto her back, but this was not the time to lose control. He needed to provide her with something more valuable than a good fucking.

"Now, Mariam," he warned. She nodded, more to herself than him, and settled across his lap. Her ass rested in a perfect place for him to access it. It spoke of experience in receiving punishment, which surprised Trace given her previously wild lifestyle. "You've done this before."

"Yes," she admitted. "But just with an opened hand. Never with anything like that." She gestured to the paddle resting on the bed beside them.

"Well, we are going to fix that today. I might use my hand for fun spankings, and even this paddle can feel good in the right way," he said, tracing her perfect globes with his finger. She sucked in a breath when he stopped and rested his hand near her wet passage. "For today, however, the paddle will be a punishment. And I trust you know why."

She nodded and hid her face in the bedsheets. Trace moved her arms and placed them both above her head, instructing her to keep them clasped together. To his pleasure and surprise, she obeyed without complaint. Maybe taming Mariam would be easier than he thought.

"I am going to spank you twenty times, Mariam. I want you to count for me and thank me for each one. There will be no more talk about this incident between us when we are finished, though I expect you to make amends with Jessica. I doubt you had to force her into participating in your ridiculous plan, but you are a leader in this pack. She should be able to rely upon you for good judgment."

Wordlessly, Mariam nodded her understanding again. She clenched her butt in anticipation of the first strike. "Shhh," he said, running his hand gently over her ass. "It will sting less if you relax, little wolf."

She followed his advice just in time to feel the first slap of the paddle. She cried out, but Trace offered her no comfort. He waited for her to remember her part in this, knowing that each strike would hurt more the longer she delayed.

"One," Mariam panted. "Thank you."

"Thank you, sir," he corrected her. Trace took another swing at her ass, enjoying the way it reddened under the heavy wood. This time, she remembered the words much faster.

"Two. Thank you, sir," she breathed against the pain. He rewarded her words by rubbing her cheeks. She sighed with relief at the contact.

The subsequent swats came faster as she learned that a quick succession inflicted less pain. By the time she said twenty and thanked him for it, her mascara was running down her face just like Jessica's had earlier. Trace pushed aside the memory of the other woman and focused entirely on his beautiful mate.

"Up on your knees," he commanded. Slightly dazed, Mariam shifted to her knees between his legs. Her tears and red ass had him so hard he thought he might burst. Trace pulled her hair back, using his hand as a tie. "Suck me, mate."

Mariam licked her lips and dove forward, eagerly stuffing as much of his dick as she could into her mouth. He groaned, feeling the resistance from her throat when she tried to take even more.

Trace gently pushed her head forward to help her deep throat him to the base. Finally, he felt the sweet pressure of her lips against his balls. She swirled her tongue over the shaft as well as she could, but he knew that his girth was making that a struggle.

She created a suction with her lips that sent him straight to heaven. He dropped her hair and leaned back on his elbows, never once breaking eye contact with her. The view of her mouth on his dick was mesmerizing. The tears were gone, but the ruined makeup made her look like a whore. *My whore.*

Our whore, his wolf corrected. He shone through Trace's eyes for a moment, eager to experience the sensation for himself, but he quickly returned to the shadows of the human's mind. This was a moment for the alpha to enjoy with his female. This was them bonding together.

Trace raised his hips to fill her, and then he pulled back out almost completely. He gave a loud groan as he found the perfect rhythm for his thrusting. The sound of wet dick and slurping filled the air. Fucking her face felt even better than he imagined.

"Fuck. That's so good, Mariam. Suck my cock, baby," he moaned. "You are such a good cocksucker."

All too soon, his balls tightened, and Trace knew that the end was near if he didn't intervene. The idea of shooting his load into her belly sent him even closer to the edge, but he wanted more. He stilled and gently pulled Mariam off his cock. She gasped, breathing deeply with her throat unobstructed.

The alpha stood and scooped her onto the bed. Her voice let out a sound of panic when he settled between her thighs.

For a moment, Trace thought that she was going to try to push him off, but she kept her hands still. "Remember, you can stop me with just a word," he said, breathing the promise into her ear.

Their eyes met, and she nodded her consent.

"Good girl. Now, your job is to tell me what you like, little wolf," he said, running his fingers through her gorgeous hair. "I want to hear all your responses to what I'm going to do to you."

"Okay, Trace," she said, swallowing hard. His eyes skimmed her throat, reminding him how she had come undone when he grabbed her there before.

The mating mark on Mariam's neck called to him, and Trace brought his lips to it, sucking and nipping gently. She began tearing at his back, desperately trying to find her release. Her nails pierced his skin when her first orgasm hit, but he didn't mind at all. Like her, the pain only brought him closer to losing control.

"Yes! Goddess, why does that feel so good. Please, I need more, Trace."

He snaked his fingers lower as she rode out her pleasure. He used his thumb to circle her clitoris, grazing against it without giving her the pressure she needed to come again.

Shoving two fingers inside her, Trace couldn't help but groan at how wet she was. he pumped them into her, mimicking what was yet to come. The fullness caused her to almost reach ecstasy again. He stopped just short of her release.

"Please," Mariam begged, thrashing as she tried to replace his fingers with her own. "Don't stop! Please!"

"Beg me for my cock," he growled at her, grasping her hand and pinning it to the bed. "I want you to beg me to fill you up."

"Please! Please fill me up," she breathed.

Her helpless plea did the trick. He lined up his cock with

her opening and pushed forward, loving how tight she felt around him. The warmth of her tunnel was almost too much for him to take.

Beneath him, Mariam screamed and shuttered with pleasure. Taking his entire length was enough to make her come almost instantly. His wolf swelled with pride; knowing that they could inspire such a reaction from her meant everything to both of them.

Trace took her second climax as permission to find his own release in her slick folds. He pulled her legs up and rested them on his shoulders to position himself even deeper inside her. He drilled in and out of his mate, loving how she screamed every time he bottomed out.

She seemed to drink up the pain that came with each thrust.

"It's too much," she cried. "Fuck, you're so big! Please, don't stop. I'm almost there!"

"I'm going to come," he warned her, hoping that she would let me finish in her pussy. He'd pull out if she told him to, but he longed to pump his seed into her. He wanted her to spread her lips afterward and show him what his jizz looked like dripping out of her used hole.

The thought of her open wide and on display emptied his balls. Trace shouted her name and let go of her legs, landing on his elbows to prevent his weight from crushing her.

Mariam's arms encircled his neck, holding him in place against her. He continued pumping into her long after he was spent, enjoying how their combined wetness felt against his cock. It was done. They were mated for life.

Chapter 17

I woke up in Trace's bed sore all over. The worst of it radiated from my behind, which was extremely tender to the touch. In the shower, it took extra care to wash without pain from the punishment blossoming anew. My pussy won second place for the most well-used areas on my body, but I had no complaints about that.

I had stayed up late into the night, long after Trace had fallen asleep, considering how different sex was with him. Comparing the memories of him and Patrick had caused him to flash angry messages to me in his sleep, which alerted me that we were now connected in that way.

I had let the matter go, ending my inner dialogue with the decision that sex with Trace was infinitely better than anything else I had experienced. The conclusion earned me a rumble of approval and his arm swinging over my hips to pull me against him.

Somehow, someway, he was already hard again. With no energy to pursue another round of mind-blowing sex, I had snuggled against his warmth and fallen into a deep sleep. The memory made me smile. I had never felt so safe and cared for. The satisfied feelings had bounced between us subconsciously as we slept.

But now, as I observed the damage Trace had done to my ass, I was tempted to turn the connection off entirely. My cheeks were deep red, almost purple in some spots. For a werewolf, that was saying a lot. *How dare he do that to me? I* demanded of my wolf.

But instead of a response for her, Trace rang clear as day in my mind. *It is my right and privilege to punish you when it is called for, little wolf. If you don't want your ass painted, I'd suggest not misbehaving again.*

I grit my teeth against my ready response, unsure if arguing would cause him to deliver another round of pain.

That unspoken question was answered, too. *No, Mariam. You are free to question anything respectfully. A spanking like that is only for severe misbehavior.*

As disconcerting as it was to have Trace in my head, there were undoubtedly bonuses. It seemed like he was able to capture the intention of my thoughts, which was highly preferred to the arguing in circles that we were used to doing.

I sighed and walked into the closet that I now shared with the alpha. He revealed that a whole new wardrobe had been delivered for me there, meaning that I could finally stop cycling through the same four outfits. I found a beautiful, soft burgundy shirt and matched it with a pair of black leggings and new boots. Everything fit perfectly, and I admired my reflection in the full-length mirror.

You make my mouth water, mate. Trace's voice filled my mind again. I turned away from the mirror and strolled back into the bedroom, where he was shamelessly sprawled across the bed naked. His hand gripped the length of his cock, and he stroked it lightly. Apparently, he had enjoyed the show in the mirror and watching me get ready.

"You're a peeper." I accused, throwing a pillow to prevent myself from shedding my clothes and climbing on top of him again. His eyes lit up as he saw my thoughts.

"Not a peeper. Just a very fortunate mate," he said, releasing himself and stretching as far as his arms would reach. I had to admit, the man's physique was impressive. He could easily take up the whole king-sized bed on his own if he tried.

"What are your plans for today?" I asked, sitting on the very edge of the mattress to avoid his hungry hands and eyes.

Trace sighed at being reminded of the reality of running a pack. "I need to debrief with Justine and Randy about yesterday. And I need to manage a few accounts with a supplier for the diner and the school cafeteria."

My heart jumped at the mention of the school. I showed him images of me working with the students there, hoping that it would be enough for him to allow me to return. His eyes softened as he viewed the scenes.

"You are going to make a wonderful mother one day, Mariam," he whispered.

Panic started to rise in my throat. That was not the response I was hoping for, and my first reaction was to stand and bolt from the room. I had no intention of being a mother any time soon. Maybe ever.

But surely, Trace would expect me to produce at least one heir. I was an idiot to think otherwise.

"Hey," Trace said gently, reaching for my hand. "I'm not in any rush to have kids, but they might happen sooner rather than later if we continue on like we did last night."

I stared back at him. I had always used a combination of the pill and condoms to prevent pregnancy in the past. But I hadn't been on birth control since running away from home, and the stickiness I felt between my legs that morning told me that Trace had forgone using protection, too.

"I see," Trace said after listening to my racing thoughts. "Well, we can take some precautions from now on. I'll wear a condom until you get back on birth control if that works for you. I love imagining my cum inside you, but I want you to feel comfortable with it."

I nodded, wanting to end the conversation quickly and not dwell on the mistakes we made the night before. Trace huffed at the idea that our lovemaking was a mistake. In my mind's eye, my wolf sided with him on the issue. She felt great being able to commune with our mate without shifting. Trace's wolf nudged her affectionately, showing his support, too.

"Can I please go back to work now?" I asked. With all the talk about having children, I had almost forgotten my purpose in showing him my classes.

Trace didn't answer right away. His jaw ticked in the way it did when he was mulling something over. After a few seconds of deliberation, he nodded. I was going to rush to hug him, but he ruined the moment with a warning.

"This is only on a day-to-day basis, Mariam," Trace said. "And I want one of my men to take you there and pick you up after dismissal."

I scowled at him. "Do you really think Tumblewild is that dangerous? If people in this pack need guards with them, that should be your biggest concern."

He narrowed his eyes at my sarcastic tone. "Watch it, mate. I said respectful questioning was fine, but you are walking a fine line with that attitude. And no, the streets are not dangerous to our pack members. We haven't had an instance of real crime in years."

"Then why can't I drive myself?" The question hung in the air between us, leaving me to answer it for him. "You don't trust me to come back home."

"I—" Trace sat up in bed, struggling to provide his feelings aloud. I probed his thoughts, trying to see if they could explain what he wanted to say. I saw him frantic, trying desperately to catch up with me in the Feldman parking lot. Then the image changed to me driving past in the truck, narrowly avoiding him in my haste. Other scenes, ones I couldn't remember, showed him smashing items against the wall and screaming in Randy's face. I caught a quick glimpse of Alexander in the hotel room before he cut me off, leaving me with just my own thoughts.

"I can't lose you again, Mariam," he whispered. My eyes watered at his desperation. I took his hand and sat beside him on the bed.

"You won't," I promised.

I smiled to myself as I put the truck in gear. Trace had been reluctant at first, but my vow to return by four-thirty was enough to allow me the freedom of going to school alone. I rolled down the window, enjoying the wind caressing my hair. My mind felt oddly empty since Trace had cut me off, but it was a welcome break. I wondered idly if sharing one consciousness felt odd for my mate, too, since he didn't appear to be in any rush to restore it.

I parked next to town hall, hoping to catch Gabe on his way to work, but I had no such luck. His empty car parked a few spaces over said that he was already inside the stately building. I grabbed my bag from the backseat and froze. A male's scent collided with my senses. It was familiar and caused my wolf to spin in circles with excitement. I stood up slowly, not believing that it was possibly him.

"Patrick," I breathed. I jumped into his arms, and he caught me easily. I hugged him tightly as though he might disappear at any minute. "How did you find me?"

He laughed deep and low. "You are the talk of Dark Claw, Mariam. At least, you are as of yesterday when Jeremy announced you were mated to the alpha of Tumblewild. You wouldn't tell me where you were the last time we spoke, so I had no way of tracking you down. I drove all night to get to you. To rescue you."

I held his face between my hands and searched for signs that I was dreaming, still not believing that he was there in front of me.

His wolf took control of his eyes, providing me with my only warning before his head dipped low to meet my lips. I instinctually closed my eyes to the familiar feeling of his mouth opening for mine, but only for an instant.

My eyes flew back open when I remembered Trace at home waiting for me. I pushed Patrick away, eager to put some distance between us.

He grabbed my ass to prevent me from falling to the ground, and I yelped in pain. He dropped his hands away and stepped back, eyes wide.

"What's wrong?" he asked, alarmed. "Did I hurt you? Did

he hurt you?"

"It's not what you think," I said, hurrying to explain before Patrick's wolf tore through him. "I was out of line, and he punished me last night."

Patrick's jaw slackened. "Since when do you consent to being punished, Mariam? That was always a hard limit when we were together, and I doubt you're really okay with crossing those boundaries with him."

I struggled to explain and defend Trace. Of course, I hadn't enjoyed the punishment, but afterward, the sex had been mind-blowing. And part of me respected him for not letting me get away with the crazy Jess situation. Patrick scowled at my loss for words.

"Don't even think about defending him, Mare. I'm getting you out of here before he has the chance to brainwash you more."

"Patrick, people are watching," I hissed. "You've got to put me down. If they saw that kiss--"

"Then they can just enjoy the view," he said, snorting to show his indifference. He grabbed my lanyard with his truck keys attached and hopped into the driver's seat. He kept me on the center seat, using his strong arm as a makeshift restraint.

"Patrick, please," I said again, this time a little louder and more firm. I wouldn't have even minded playing hooky with him for the day, but if it got back to Trace that he had kissed and manhandled me, I knew that this wasn't going to end well. I wasn't worried about effectively being kidnapped; Patrick wasn't going to hurt me, and I had no doubt he would return me home before my curfew once I explained the situation.

"Patrick, nothing," he answered, pulling out of the parking space. "I don't know what he's done to you, Mariam, but the girl I love values her freedom too much to settle for a game of whips and chains for the rest of her life."

The girl he loves? I frowned. "Patrick, we're best friends, but you aren't in love with me. You're waiting for your true mate, remember?"

The driver's side was quiet for several beats, but I didn't fill the silence. I stared him down, daring him to challenge what we both knew was the truth.

"Maybe I just needed some time to understand how little that actually matters, Mariam," he said. "Since the day you left, all I've thought about is you. I want you with me every day. I don't care if you take other lovers. I don't care if you won't let me spank you. I don't care about any of it. I just want you."

Everything felt like it was happening so fast. If Patrick had said all this a few days earlier, I would have found a way back to him so that he could bite and claim me. But none of what he said mattered anymore. "He's claimed me, Patrick. Trace bit me like I already told you, and last night we finished the mating bond. It's done. I belong to him now."

Patrick swerved over the double yellow line at that news, causing a trucker going the opposite way to honk angrily at us.

"You're lying," Patrick choked. "If you were already mated, he would be able to see everything that has happened. He would be on his way to you now, and you wouldn't give two shits about the people watching us on the sidewalk."

I shifted uncomfortably on the hard bench seat. "He

blocked me out this morning. I was seeing something in his mind that he didn't want me to see, so he severed the connection and hasn't put it back in place."

"What was he trying to prevent you from seeing?" Patrick asked. His arm stayed firmly planted against me as though I might bound out the door at any moment.

"It was Alexander. What he did to him at the hotel on the night we met, I mean."

"No wonder he didn't want you to see that," Patrick growled. "It shows him for what he is: a hot-tempered monster."

I couldn't argue with that. The memory, even the small part I saw, was terrifying and would make anyone second-guess how stable Trace truly was. If he had shown it to me before mating, I might have tried to scale out the window in my bedroom to escape.

"It's fine. That doesn't matter, either," Patrick said, bringing the conversation back to my mating bond and tearing me away from my thoughts. "There has to be something we can do, and in the meantime, I'm getting you as far away from Tumblewild as I can. If Trace can turn off your connection, so can you. Shut him out so he won't be able to see where we're going."

I considered his request and finally nodded in agreement. "I'll cut him off, Patrick, but not because I don't want to go back to him. I'll cut him off so that he won't track me down and murder you."

––––––––

The morning had dragged on, first with the crumby update about the Sweetwater pack from Randy and then an awkward visit to Jess's house to help set things right with her. The interaction had been uncomfortable at best, and Trace sincerely hoped that one day their friendship could return to normal.

They had shared a grin when she mentioned that at least he had been wearing a towel, which gave him some hope for the future. Despite her protests, Trace promised that Mariam would also be visiting her soon to express her sincere apologies.

The worst part of the whole day was maintaining the block against his connection with his mate. Trace's wolf was pacing again, in much the same way he had when Mariam was running from them. He longed for the intimacy they shared last night and this morning until the alpha had to cut it off abruptly.

Although Mariam had never claimed to have feelings for the bastard at the hotel, even Trace wasn't cruel enough to show her his final moments. And once it was done, he had decided to keep it in place until after his meeting with Jess to help spare them both additional embarrassment, but now he would be able to join her again.

He concentrated on the part of his mind that she had begun to occupy and unlocked the door that he used to shut her out. His breath caught painfully in his chest when he saw only darkness on the other side. She should be there, along with her wolf. But now, there was nothing.

His wolf whined, stressed not to be reunited with their mate. Trace's mind jumbled as he tried to make sense of it. *Was she hurt? Dead? No, I'd be able to feel the loss if she was truly gone from this world. Did she block me out herself?*

He frowned. Why would she try to keep him out of her

mind while she worked at the school? Was there something going on there? He started the truck and tried to call her phone over Bluetooth. He listened eagerly as it rang while he sped downtown to the school. Eventually, the phone hung up because she wasn't answering and hadn't set up her voicemail.

Trace dialed Randy next, anger starting to build in him. If there was an emergency and she had left her phone at home, he was going to tan her hide. She would regret causing him this much panic.

"Randy," his beta answered.

"Where's Mariam?" Trace growled. "Something's wrong with our connection, and she's not answering her phone."

Randy paused, but only for a moment. "I thought you said she was working at the school today."

"She is," he spat. "At least, she said she was working there today."

"You didn't have one of the guys drop her off?" Randy asked. The question rubbed Trace the wrong way.

"No. I trust my mate." The words were icy, but at this point, he was beginning to question his own intelligence in allowing her to go alone. She wasn't leaving him, that much he knew. Her kiss and promise this morning to return to him were solid. But if someone, an outsider, had entered pack lands and harmed her, he would never forgive himself.

What's worse, he had been the one to sever their connection, making it so she was unable to call out to him for help.

Trace slammed his hand against the steering wheel in frustration at his stupidity and selfishness. He should have lifted the veil as soon as the memory of the Feldman Hotel had passed. Sparing her the awkwardness of meeting with Jess and the intricacies of their relationship with Sweetwater wasn't worth this.

He parked hastily on Main Street, not caring whether he was inside the lines. A quick sweep of the other parked cars said she probably wasn't at the school, but Trace forced himself to believe that maybe she just parked around the corner.

The alpha stalked to the elementary school and buzzed to be let in. Heather Carpenter, the secretary at the front office, unlocked the door from her desk.

"Alpha, it's good to see you today," she said cheerily, though concern was etched on her face. "Is there something I can help you with?"

He forced himself to calm down. It wouldn't do any good to scare Heather. "I'm here to speak with my mate, Ms. Carpenter. Will you please page her down here?"

Heather looked away to focus her concentration on the floor in front of her. "I'm sorry, alpha, but Mrs. Everett isn't here. She…didn't clock in this morning."

His blood ran cold as she confirmed his worst fears, but there was still something she wasn't telling him. Trace tilted her chin up and forced her to look him in the eye. "What else do you know, Heather?"

She swallowed hard before answering. "There's been talk, alpha. Some of the teachers saw her park across the street. They were excited to see her back, so they waited for her on the sidewalk." He waited for her to continue, not moving a single muscle. "And, well… they saw a man, a male werewolf, come up behind her. At first, they thought that he might just be a friend. He isn't from our pack. But then…well, sir, they say that she jumped into his arms and kissed him. Then he carried her back into the car, and they left together."

193

Trace tried hard to restrain himself when Heather Carpenter told him what she had heard. Whatever happened, it wasn't her fault, and he didn't want to take out his panic on an innocent member of the pack. He asked her to call Randy on his behalf and have the beta meet him at the school. He also told her to set up a conference room and collect the teachers who saw his mate leave. He needed to speak with them directly.

He left her to fulfill his requests and went outside to take a closer look around Main Street. If the male wolf had taken Mariam away in the truck she drove, there was probably a car parked on the street that didn't belong to a pack member.

Deep down, Trace knew who it must be: Mariam's old fuckboy, Patrick. Images of that asshole being intimate with his mate had entered his mind only last night as Mariam had compared the quality of her encounters.

At the time, he had only cringed, hoping that she would gain a little more awareness that they were now sharing a consciousness. Trace's wolf had gone berserk over the memory, calming only a fraction when she assured them that sex was undeniably better with her true mate. He had clung to her words, praying that they were true. Their lovemaking had been earth-shattering, at least for him.

He caught Patrick's scent on an old truck tucked back on the other side of town hall. Trace recognized it instantly as the vehicle that had been parked outside Mariam's house back at Dark Claw. The fucker must have driven it here in hopes of convincing her to leave with him.

What if she wanted to leave with him?

The thought spread like poison in his mind. Desperate to combat it, Trace focused on the last conversation he had with Mariam that morning. He had been transparent about his need for her, and she had promised to return to him. Had it all been a sham? That might be the only conclusion that made sense, considering how she had blocked him out of her mind. Why would she do that if she had been taken against her will?

None of it made any sense, and meeting with the teachers didn't help, either. Their stories mirrored what Heather had already told him. They couldn't even say for sure whether Mariam had gotten into the truck of her own volition. When Randy asked if she seemed to consent to the kiss, their answers had been a meek but definitive, yes.

Upon hearing that, the beta quickly thanked and dismissed them to return to their classes. His eyes had been on Trace, waiting for an explosion of some sort the instant they were alone, but it never came. Instead, he slumped back in his chair at a loss for words.

Trace's wolf was ready to go find her the instant he learned she was missing, and he growled at his human's lack of urgency. He knew all he needed to know about

Mariam's wolf; nothing could convince him that her animal would willingly desert them.

Trace smiled sadly, thinking of the time they had spent together running with the pack. That had hands down been the best night of his wolf's entire life, perhaps only competing with the way he felt being able to join her in their collective subconscious.

He agreed with his animal right away; Mariam's wolf would never leave them willingly. But Mariam herself? The woman he had chased across the country? She gave him pause.

"What do you want to do, boss?" Randy asked, leaning against the wall, and giving Trace a wary look.

"What?" he snapped. The question had broken him out of his trance and unleashed the anger within the alpha. "Let me guess. You're too tired to track your alpha female across state lines again? You want to stay home and play house with my sister instead?"

Randy narrowed his eyes, matching his energy. "I'll let that one pass, Everett, but keep Justine out of this. That's the only warning I'll give you about that."

Trace slammed a fist down on the wood conference table, cracking it down the center. His hand ached from the impact that would have shattered a human's bones, but he ignored it. He straightened after a moment, remembering where he was and hoping that none of the classes had been disturbed by the noise.

"Forgive me," he said, genuinely sorry. "What should I do, beta?"

"Honestly, I don't know what I would do," Randy said, coming up beside him and examining his injured hand.

"From what I could tell, Mariam loved living in Tumblewild. Gabe told me she wanted to join the pack long before she knew you were part of it. She has made some good friends here, and she even allowed you to complete the mating bond, right? Something just doesn't make sense."

Trace frowned. Randy was right; if Mariam had planned on leaving that morning, she would have never had sex with him last night. What was the purpose of sealing their bond if she just wanted to leave? Could it be that she just wanted to give him a false sense of security? Or maybe her hormones had gotten the best of her, and she regretted it later?

He closed his eyes at the thought, hating the possibility that Mariam hadn't really wanted to be with him. But no— that didn't make sense, either. He had been able to see and feel her genuine thoughts that morning.

Plus, she didn't know he was going to let her go to work until after breakfast, just moments before she left. Had her boyfriend been on standby for days, just waiting for her to slip away?

Trace had no answer for that, but maybe her former alpha would know. "Get Jeremy from Dark Claw on the line," he said.

Patrick didn't stop until we reached the hotel several hours later. Trace had made sure I had a full tank of gas before seeing me off that morning, which had unintentionally allowed for an easier escape. We didn't have any luggage to carry other than my purse, leaving Patrick free to grab me by the hand. It felt wrong, not only as a mated she-wolf but also because it was something we had never done before. I had to wonder if he was afraid of me trying to run away or if he was just being weirdly affectionate.

"Hello, ma'am," he greeted the woman at the front desk. "We have a reservation under the name Patrick Callahan."

She looked the information up on her computer and smiled at our hands joined together, but her face quickly filled with concern when she spotted the mating bite on my neck. While most female wolves liked to display them proudly, mating marks were also known to alarm humans, who had no way of differentiating them from a sign of abuse.

"Thanks, babe," I said to Patrick, smiling and hoping that the endearment was enough to ease the woman's mind. I might not be mated to him, but I also didn't want the human police involved. "It was thoughtful of you to reserve a room for us."

Patrick's eyes widened, and then he smiled back, giving my hand a squeeze. He leaned in for a kiss, but I covered my mouth and turned away, pretending to cough. I sincerely hoped that he wasn't reading into what I said.

Thankfully, the human processed his request and gave him the papers to sign without issue. We found the elevator and took it up to the fourth floor. I was in awe of how ornate it was; everything was made of glass and faux gold, giving us glamorous views of the lobby and casino below.

My eyes widened when we walked through the door. The room was massive, and the view of the Las Vegas strip was breathtaking. I shot Patrick a judgmental glance when I spied the bouquet of flowers and the two-person, heart-shaped tub. No wonder the receptionist had given us those looks.

"Is this a honeymoon suite, Patrick?"

He gave me a sheepish look. "I didn't know how...excited you'd be about leaving, okay? I thought you might want to celebrate. We don't have to do anything if you're not ready."

I sighed and grabbed the bottle of champagne off the coffee table. There was a basket of fruit and chocolate that looked a little tempting, too, but I would focus my attention on the alcohol first.

The cork opened with a loud *pop!*, releasing a stream of bubbles. I caught most of the fizz with my hand and quickly brought my fingers to my lips. I closed my eyes, enjoying the sweet carbonation. Suddenly, Patrick was by my side. He ran a finger down the side of the bottle and took it from my hands.

"Mind if I have a taste?" he whispered, tucking my hair behind my ear. I gasped at the innuendo and spun around to glare at him, but he had already brought the bottle to his mouth. His eyes danced with laughter at the joke.

"Idiot," I said, smacking him on the arm and stealing the champagne back. I took a long drink and passed it to him. "So, how long are you keeping me prisoner here, Patrick? Can I at least call Trace? He's probably really worried if he knows that I'm not at the school."

Patrick sighed and took a long drink. "When you say things like that, it reminds me of how not okay you are right now, Mare. I'm guessing he broke something in you, and I want to rip his head off for that. But I'm no dummy; I know he'd pulverize me in a fight and take you prisoner, again, so the best I can do is get you as far away from him as possible."

"So, your plan is to what? Keep me locked away forever?" I asked.

"No, not forever. Just however long it takes to help you remember who you are and what you want," he answered. "Look at it this way, Mare. This is me fulfilling a promise to a friend. I couldn't stop him from taking you from Dark Claw that day. The way you screamed my name when he carried you off still gets to me."

Patrick's eyes clouded over, almost like he was living through it again. I scooted over to him and rested my head on his shoulder, wanting to comfort him. "A lot has changed since then. That was over a month ago," I reminded him.

"Yeah, but your call telling me that all hope was lost and that he had basically forced you into a mating bite was only a few days ago," he countered. "Whatever he did to make you change your mind, it's only happened recently. You'll see. Maybe you'll even want me to break his claim on you…you know, give you a new bite and become your mate. The sex wouldn't be too bad, either. We always did well in that department together, right?"

His voice sounded so hopeful, and it was breaking my heart. "Patrick, that's not possible. And even if it was, I want you to experience the true mate thing for yourself. It's pretty amazing, I have to say."

"We'll see," he said. "Let's give it a few days and see how you feel."

We quickly polished off the bottle of champagne and sampled a few pieces of fruit. Since we were at an impasse, there was no reason to continue arguing about contacting Trace.

I always had the option of lifting the barrier to see if he was there, but I also didn't want him to be privy to my thoughts. If he knew that Patrick had taken me across state lines to Vegas and booked us a honeymoon suite, his fate would be set. All I wanted was a way to contact him and let him know that I was safe. *And that you haven't abandoned him,* my wolf added from where she was hiding in the shadows.

Yeah, that, too.

"So, what do you want to do with your new-found freedom?" Patrick asked as we raided the minibar. I frowned as he downed a few mini bottles of vodka.

"I'm not sure, but you better take it easy," I said. "I have enough to cover the room and this stuff, by the way. I still need to repay you all the money you lent me."

I grabbed my purse and pulled out an envelope stuffed with cash. Patrick's eyes widened. It was almost all the money I had earned from working at the school, minus what I needed to spend for my phone and food while living with Gabe. I had decided not to spend it and instead give it to Patrick when he came to pick up his truck. That time had come a lot sooner than I thought.

"Jeez, Mariam. How much is that? I didn't give you that much, not by a long shot."

"Almost two thousand dollars," I said, shrugging. "Consider the extra as interest and a thank you."

I tried to hand it to him, but he wouldn't take it. "I appreciate that you want to do this, but you don't have to pay me back. We can put this money to good use, Mariam. This is enough for us to rent a place, at least for a month or two, until we can find new jobs. This is enough to start over with, Mare."

I sighed. "We've already argued about this enough for one day. We're both a little tipsy, and I don't feel like fighting. Let's go take a walk or something. I've never been to the strip."

Patrick nodded and helped me to my feet, though he was the one who seemed to have a hard time keeping his balance. I stifled a grin, remembering some of our other alcohol-induced nights together.

Even though it was the middle of a weekday, Vegas was alive with lights, sounds, and people. A man old enough to be my father came out of a casino and gave me an appreciative whistle that made me want to gag. One glare from Patrick had sent the man packing. The exchange seemed to disturb my friend up a bit, and after that, he kept a protective arm draped across my shoulders as we walked. "Tell me how everyone is doing," I said. "How is Ella? And Lance?"

"I think Ella's good. I saw her at the pack run a few nights back. She seemed a little closed off, like she didn't want to talk, so I didn't approach her. And Lance is the same as always. He was pretty fucked up when he found out that you called me and not him."

I frowned, feeling guilty that I didn't know Lance's phone number by heart. Patrick grinned at me, making me realize that the only way Lance would even know I called him was if he had rubbed it in.

I elbowed him, once again amazed at the competition between the two men who had sworn up and down that they'd have no problems sharing a girlfriend.

"Do you still have your phone?" I asked, changing the subject.

"Yeah, I needed it for the GPS to get to Flagstaff," Patrick said. "Why?"

I rolled my eyes at him. "Jeremy put all that tracking stuff on our phones, remember? If you don't want him to know where you are, you should probably get rid of it."

Patrick's eyes widened. He quickly fished his phone out of his pocket and took off the back. "What should I do, Mare? Is there something I can just easily remove?"

I shrugged. I wasn't very tech-savvy either. Patrick sighed and wrapped his hand around the phone, crushing it like it was a flimsy piece of paper. He broke it in a couple of different places until he felt confident that it was completely dead. We continued walking together, and he dumped it in a trash can as we went by.

"How is Jeremy?" I asked. "Did he blame you for helping me get away?"

"Jeremy was pretty pissed for a long time," Patrick admitted. "I thought for a while he might banish me. I guess Trace Everett was breathing down his neck hard about it, so he mainly just wanted me to tell him where you were hiding. He was bent out of shape when I could honestly say that I didn't know. What made you go to Tumblewild?"

"I thought maybe I could join a pack and start a new life until it was safe to come home. Tumblewild was open to visitors and I had enough money to get there. Those are the only reasons, really. What are the odds of it being Trace's pack, right?"

"Yeah, what are the odds?" Patrick said softly.

On our walk, we encountered some street performers and crazy-looking humans. We decided to eat dinner at one of the low-priced buffets, which turned out to be surprisingly good.

Neither of us had any desire to gamble, but we did stop at the liquor store before going back to the hotel. It felt right to loosen up with some alcohol while we were in Sin City, and I had my own motivations for encouraging Patrick to drink.

An hour later, after he had downed several more shots of vodka, Patrick sprawled out on the bed, snoring. I took a key card and left the room, praying that he wouldn't wake up until after I returned. Downstairs, I went straight to the reception counter. The same woman from earlier was there, and she seemed to remember me.

"Hi, ma'am. You checked me and my…um, *husband…* in a little while ago, and I was just wondering if I could make a phone call. It would be long-distance, but I can pay for it."

Her eyes traveled to my scar again, and for once, I was thankful for the distrustful nature of humans. "I'm not really supposed to do this, but you can use my cell phone," she said, reaching behind the counter and grabbing it from her bag. "Don't worry about it being long-distance. It makes no difference on my plan."

"Thanks so much," I said. I looked at the phone for a moment and then felt extremely foolish. I didn't know Trace's number. I didn't know anyone's number from the Tumblewild pack by heart. I bit on my lip and handed the woman back her phone. "On second thought, I don't need to make a call after all. Thanks anyway, though."

This seemed to concern her even more, but I sped off, not wanting to come up with another lie. Using the word "husband" to describe Patrick had left a bitter taste in my mouth. I was done with all of this. I just wanted Trace to come and take me home. I'd be able to protect Patrick from whatever rage my mate projected when he arrived.

I found a quiet spot by the indoor fountain and closed my eyes, searching for a way to open the door I had closed on him. Finally, I found it. Part of me expected to see the darkness that had been there when my mate shut me out, but instead, I saw that he was in a car, riding in the passenger's seat.

Trace?

Mariam? I felt my mate's relief flood through him. *Where are you? Why did you leave?*

I sighed, knowing that he'd have a lot of questions I would need to answer. *I didn't want to leave. A friend thought I was in danger and came to get me. It was a misunderstanding.*

I hadn't had as much to drink as Patrick, but the alcohol in my system lowered my inhibitions, and I started showing Trace images and scenes of what had happened. Once it started, I couldn't stop them from coming. The ones where Patrick flirted with me and offered to become my new mate earned him a threatening growl from Trace, but by the end, my mate seemed to understand the situation better.

I'm in Las Vegas, I told him.

I know, Trace answered. *Randy and I are almost there, maybe an hour away. Your boyfriend was too dumb to realize that your former alpha could track his phone.*

Relief flooded through me at the thought of seeing Trace and going home. He rumbled his approval, sharing my feelings. Our wolves were back together, as well, curled up and content to be reunited.

I frowned, remembering how quiet my wolf had gotten over the whole ordeal. She had only spoken a time or two, and I had been so preoccupied with Patrick that I hadn't stopped to consider why she was silent.

She was probably confused. She knows your friend as an ally but is also loyal to my wolf. She'll be fine, Mariam.

There was only one thing left worrying me. *Promise me that you won't harm Patrick,* I begged.

Trace didn't answer verbally but instead unloaded a cascade of emotions on me. I sighed. Maybe some discussions were better to have in person.

Chapter 19

I sat at the fountain for a while, savoring being back in Trace's company. Now that he knew I was safe and that I hadn't tried to escape from him, he was in a much better mood. He was, dare I say, even a little playful?

We have an approximate location of your hotel based upon cell towers, and now that I can see your surroundings, I know exactly where you are. I've actually stayed in that hotel before. My wolf yipped with the knowledge that our mate would be able to find us. She was more than ready to return home and leave the loud and confusing city behind.

Trace's wolf licked her face, mirroring her happiness. Despite the adorable scene unfolding before us, a wicked smile grew across my mate's face. *I bet I'll be able to find you from your scent alone when I arrive. Care to make a wager on it, Mariam?*

My heart pounded in my chest at the thought of Trace tracking me throughout the hotel. He might be right about the whole scent thing; it was basically a beacon for mates to find each other, but I would give him a run for his money. *You're on.*

He grinned at the challenge. *I'll be there in about ten minutes if you want to run and hide in your room. If you stay where you are, I'll find you in no time. Besides, half of the fun will be collecting my winnings as soon as I lay eyes on you. Being alone in your room will make that much easier.* Trace tried to throw sexy ideas into my head, but I was too focused on what he said.

I frowned- ten minutes? How had so much time passed?

I'm going to need to turn off our connection again, Trace.

No, he said flatly. His wolf barked, echoing his dissent.

I have to warn Patrick. I don't want him to wake up and find me gone with no explanation. Besides…we were sharing a room.

Trace fumed. It was quickly apparent that sharing that information had been the wrong choice.

I'll deal with him when I get there. But you, little wolf, if you shut me out again, there will be hell to pay. The threat made me pause, but only for a moment. I felt the pull to submit, and it took every ounce of my willpower to overcome it. The only thing that saved me was trying to think logically. Chances were, I was already in some hot water for severing the connection earlier. I might as well do what needed to be done and face the consequences later.

Trace snarled at my thoughts, eager to set me straight, but before he could, I shut the door between us and locked it. My wolf and I were alone again in my mind's eye.

I rode the beautiful elevator up to the room, this time not bothering to admire it. My heart started to pound when I got off on the fourth floor. Werewolf metabolisms were no joke; his body had probably already burned through all the alcohol. He must have woken up to find me gone and lost control.

I ran down the hall, hoping that he wasn't trying to claw

his way out through the door. Thankfully, when I got there, it was still in one piece. I fumbled with the key card until finally, the door opened, and I was greeted with a few hundred pounds of overjoyed werewolf fluff.

I smiled fondly at Patrick's wolf as he celebrated my return. I ran my fingers over his coat, stroking its silky softness. I was grateful to see him again in that form. It had been too long since our last run together.

And as much as I hated to admit it, I probably wouldn't be seeing Patrick again after this. Trace would never trust me to spend time with him, and I knew I wasn't going to be able to defy my mate on such a big issue. I was already feeling the strain caused by disobeying him and shutting off our connection, even though I knew it was the right thing to do for Patrick's sake.

My wolf howled at the idea of losing our friend again. "Hey, can you shift back? I need to talk to your human," I whispered to the oversized puppy.

Within seconds, Patrick appeared before me in human form.

"Why did you leave?" he demanded, eyes flashing. "I woke up, and you were gone. My wolf forced the shift, Mariam. Do you realize how painful that is?"

"Sorry," I said sheepishly, trying to look away from Patrick's naked body. "I know you didn't want me to do it, but I needed to tell Trace I was okay and that I wanted to go home to him. I reestablished the connection, and I found out they were already on their way here."

Patrick froze. "Are you telling me that Trace Everett is staring at me right now, in all my naked glory?"

I giggled at the thought. "No, I closed that door before I

came back so I could tell you what's going on in private."

"Here's to small blessings, I guess," Patrick said, sitting back down on the bed. "So, this is really over then, huh, Mare?"

I nodded sadly. "Are you going back to Dark Claw? I'm pretty sure Trace's pack wouldn't mind if I just left with you, to be honest. They probably all think I'm crazy for running from him twice."

Patrick snorted and reached for my hand. "They're your pack now, too, Mariam. Honestly, I'm kind of jealous that you know what you want out of life. I thought we would be together, at least as friends, but I guess--"

He was cut off by Trace's bellows from the hallway. I paled, my eyes wide as I looked at Patrick. He was sitting on the bed with a pillow on his lap but was otherwise still completely nude. "You've got to get dressed!"

"My wolf tore through my clothes when he forced the shift," he answered sheepishly. "I left Dark Claw in a hurry and didn't really pack anything else."

"Mariam!' Trace pounded on the door. "You have thirty seconds to open this door, or I'm coming through it." It wasn't an idle threat. Memories of him shattering the guest bedroom door were firmly planted in my mind.

"Just a minute!" I hollered back. Turning to Patrick, I gave my friend one chance of survival. "I'll see if there's anything you could wear at the gift shop. You need to shift back, so my mate doesn't start breathing fire when I let him in."

Patrick gave a short nod, and the sound of his bones setting again filled the room. Soon, the silky black wolf reappeared at my side. I gave him a scratch behind the ears and stood to face the music.

"I'm opening the door, Trace," I said loudly. I wasn't sure why I felt the need to warn him, but I did it anyway. I turned the handle, my eyes lighting up as soon as I saw him standing there.

His first reaction was to pull me to him, holding me so tight that I couldn't take deep breaths. His hand felt my hair and tilted my face upward to study my eyes.

"I swear to the moon goddess, wayward mate if you ever—"

"I won't," I promised, reaching around his neck to pull him down for a kiss. There was an urgency as he claimed my mouth that caused a heavy tug in my lower stomach. It continued to spread, heating my sex from within and setting my body on fire. From the hallway, Randy cleared his throat, stepping around us and into the room.

"Good to see you in one piece, Mariam," he said, taking in the room around him. I untangled myself enough from my mate to turn and look at the other man.

Trace's arm remained fully planted across my chest, holding my behind firmly against his front. I could feel his hardness as it jutted against my ass. I wiggled a little, which did little to ease his predicament.

What did help was him surveying the room with his beta. The honeymoon suite felt even more ridiculous with all three men in the room.

"Care to explain all of this, Mariam?" Trace asked, gesturing to the couple's tub and single bed.

"I'm sure it's the only room that was available," I answered, unable to contain my laughter. My mate's eyes remained hard, but his lips twitched. We never even made it an entire night, and the bed and Jacuzzi we both obviously unused. Besides, my thoughts had already revealed that nothing had happened between us, and the only scent from Patrick I carried came from his wolf.

Randy eyed the animal with a quizzical expression. "Why is he in wolf form? Is he too scared to face us as a man or something?"

Patrick's wolf growled at the jab, wanting to assert himself as an equal to the beta. I scowled on his behalf, too. Patrick wasn't a coward.

"No," I huffed. "His wolf forced a shift when he woke up, and I wasn't here. He was wearing the only clothes he had, and we thought wolf form would be better than straight-up nudity. Or should he change back?"

Trace squeezed me tighter, and the sound of disapproval vibrated in his chest. Randy nodded his understanding. "I'll go see what I can find for him."

I gave him an appreciative smile. I wasn't really sure where I stood with Randy personally, but he seemed to always pull through when he was needed.

There was only one thing left to do: I closed my eyes and restored the mental connection between Trace and me. My wolf spun in circles before tackling her mate. She playfully nipped at his ears, trying to get him to chase her. He howled and took off after her.

"He'll catch her soon enough," the alpha of Tumblewild whispered in my ear. "And you owe me a prize for winning our bet and tracking you down in this hotel. It was way too easy. Your intoxicating scent brought me right to this spot."

I felt myself start to melt again, but I stopped short when I remembered that Patrick was still in the room. While the human would have probably given us privacy long before now, the wolf was more curious about our exchange. He tilted his head as though our words were odd to him. Of course, he wasn't privy to the things we shared between our minds. I wondered if the animal even knew how Trace and I connected mentally, having never experienced it for himself.

"Let's get out of here," Trace said, reaching down behind my knees and pulling me into the air to carry me out. He let the door slam behind him.

For some reason, I found it inexplicably hilarious that Patrick would need to shift to open the door for Randy and receive his new clothes. I wondered if the beta would just hand them over or toy with the naked werewolf a little. And then there was the matter of the sleeping arrangements that night.

Trace grinned at the thought of our two best friends sharing the honeymoon suite. I couldn't wait to fill Justine in on what happened when we returned home.

"Harder," I pleaded, trying my best not to broadcast my desire to the other patrons of the hotel. Being able to feel my mate's pleasure, as well as my own, was almost too much to handle. My reactions were probably going to get us kicked out of our room.

"But I love to hear you scream," Trace whispered, leaning forward so I could feel his warm breath on my neck. He gave me what I asked for and started pounding into me with increased vigor. "Scream for me, mate."

His command was my undoing, and I cried out my release. The mental connection we shared gave us both a taste of how the orgasm felt for me and combined it with the effect it had on his body.

Trace shifted his weight and clapped a hand over my mouth to muffle the sound of my ecstasy. My arms gave out from under me, but my ass stayed in the air. From Trace's view above, I could see that his handprints on my backside were still visible, a fact that he found most satisfying.

My mate grabbed a fistful of my hair with his free hand, using it to force my face harder into the mattress. It was a little degrading how he pounded me into the bed, almost acting as if I was just a vessel for his desire.

I whimpered at his assault on my pussy, not sure how much longer I could accommodate him taking me from behind.

"You'll take it until I finish. You'll take it like a whore. You are my whore, aren't you, Mariam?"

I shook with another orgasm, surprised by how the combination of punishment, rough sex, and name-calling affected me. I had always been sensitive about being thought of as a whore, but the way Trace said it hit me differently. I was, in all ways, eager and willing to be his whore.

My mind drifted, and I started floating. I wasn't having another orgasm, but it felt like my body was alive for the first time. I was vaguely aware when Trace grunted his release. He held onto my hips, pumping his seed into the condom until he finally pulled out and discarded it into the waste bin.

He slipped into the bed beside me, pulling my shaking body to him. The feeling of flying was still going strong, and I blinked a few times, trying to focus on his face.

"Shhhh, little wolf," he said, tucking my head under his chin. "Welcome to subspace, mate."

I smoothed the front of my white dress and checked my reflection one more time in the full-length mirror. I had shut Trace out of my mind again, but at least this time, it wouldn't earn me a trip over his knee. Everyone knew that it was bad luck to see the bride before the ceremony, and the last thing we needed was to start off our marriage with that hanging over our heads.

Never in my wildest dreams did I imagine I would be taking part in a human mating ceremony —a wedding— of all things. But ever since Trace caught wind of the fact that I had referred to Patrick as my husband to the hotel receptionist, he had been dead set on us getting married before going home to Tumblewild.

His reasoning was that if I was going to call anyone husband, it was going to be him. He had also taken to referring to me as his bride while interacting with humans during our stay in Las Vegas.

Getting married in Sin City was probably the most cliche thing we could do, but Trace wanted it done fast so we could focus more time and resources on our mating ceremony, where we would invite our packmates, friends, and family to celebrate our bond. A mating ceremony was the werewolf way, but my wolf was equally happy to take part in this, as well. She wanted to be his; heart, body, and soul. I couldn't disagree with that.

The engagement ring Trace had given me earlier that day glimmered on my finger, making me smile. He hadn't known about that tradition until Patrick mentioned it to him over breakfast, causing a last-minute trip to the jewelry store.

One day I would have to thank him for helping my mate select the perfect setting. While neither of them was particularly fond of the other, it seemed like Trace and Patrick had reached some kind of truce.

There was a brief knock at the door, and Patrick slipped inside to join me in the bridal suite without waiting for an invitation. I knew that normally human women had a maid of honor, which probably would have been Ella in other circumstances, but I liked having Patrick by my side even more. He had seen me through so much, sometimes to his own detriment.

"Are you ready, Mariam?" he asked, his eyes sweeping over me and taking in the beauty of the dress. I had to admit, pointless human tradition or not, the gown was gorgeous.

"I think so," I said, reaching for his hand. "You know, in a way, Trace should be thanking you for all of this. We wouldn't be getting married if you hadn't gone rogue and kidnapped me."

"You should absolutely point that out to him sometime," he said, pulling me in for a chaste hug. "If you're happy, I'm happy for you, Mare. That's all that's ever mattered to me. You know that, right?"

I leaned my head against his chest, listening to his heartbeat and knowing without question that his words rang true. I felt tears well in my eyes, but I forced them back. My makeup had taken way too long to ruin it before things even got started. "I *am* happy, and now it's time for you to find your own happiness, Patrick. Just promise you'll come and visit me, okay?"

He chuckled, the sound rumbling through his chest. I smiled, but my eyes remained misty. I would miss him.

"Shall we?" Patrick offered me his arm, and I accepted it. Together we crossed the threshold of the chapel. The room was stunning, but my eyes went straight to the man who had successfully tracked me down not once but twice. When he saw me for the first time, the look on his face said he considered it worth the wait.

The bonfire crackled, releasing a ribbon of smoke that swirled above our heads. I snuggled in closer to Trace, enjoying the warmth from the flames and his arms wrapped around me. He kissed the top of my head and rumbled contently. After a pack run and a delicious meal of barbeque ribs, there was an air of satisfaction shared with everyone around us.

"I could stay like this forever," I said. "Maybe we should have pack runs every other week instead of once a month."

"You do a lot of the planning, so that's entirely up to you, Mariam," Trace answered. "I doubt anyone would argue with you about it."

"Every week would be even better," Justine agreed. She set down her plate and curled up on Randy's lap.

Our mating ceremony was quickly approaching and overseeing the logistics for the pack run had been a welcome distraction. Surprisingly, there were quite a few Dark Claw pack members who would be joining us for the big day.

Jeremy would have to be present as my former alpha, but I was a little surprised that Patrick, Lance, and Ella also RSVP'd to attend. I had only spoken to my sister once since getting married to Trace.

The conversation had been short and surprisingly awkward, with her making up an excuse to end the call without offering any kind of congratulations to us. I had to wonder if she was only coming to the ceremony out of a sense of obligation. She didn't seem too happy about the fact that I was content and mated before her.

Maybe she isn't sure what to say over the phone and wants to celebrate with you in person, Trace offered through our connection.

Maybe we should just elope again, I countered. *It worked out well enough for the wedding in Vegas.*

Trace agreed, sending me his memories of watching me walk down the aisle to him. Unfortunately, there was no werewolf equivalent for a small mating ceremony; it was meant to be celebrated by the whole pack.

It was even more essential for us to host all the members of Tumblewild at the ceremony because it was when I would become an official alpha of the pack, holding as much influence over their lives as Trace.

The night grew short, and some of the younger pack members started to help with the clean-up while the elders headed back to their homes. I spotted Gabe from where he was helping to break down the changing room tents and walked over to him.

He looked deep in thought but smiled a greeting when I offered him a hand.

"Did you enjoy the run?" I asked.

Gabe nodded as he folded a length of canvas and shoved it back in its box. "My wolf needed it. He's been a little out of sorts lately."

I frowned. "What do you mean? Is he alright?"

"I think so. It's more like he senses something. It's hard to describe."

"Well, I can't say I've had that feeling before," I said honestly. "Maybe you should talk to someone? Maybe the pack physician?"

"It's probably nothing. I'm sure he's just restless."

Trace came to assist us, and we quickly broke down the last few tents.

I walked with him hand-in-hand back to the alpha house, my mind still concerned over what Gabe had shared.

I asked Trace about it, wondering if maybe it was something he had experienced before, too.

"Actually," he said. "I had something similar happen right before leaving to visit Dark Claw. I was there originally to meet with Jeremy and discuss a possible trade agreement, but my wolf was really out of sorts. I couldn't get him to focus on anything."

"Do you think he could have sensed that we would be in the same place? Is that even possible?" I asked. Trace had never shared that bit of information with me. I had the feeling that he never even considered it himself.

"Could be," he said thoughtfully. "He had never acted like that before."

The thought made me smile. With any luck, maybe my friend would soon be finding his true mate, too.

Author's Note

I sincerely hope you enjoyed reading Mariam and Trace's unconventional love story as much as I did while writing it. There is more to come in this series, and I have much more planned for other paranormal romances, as well as additional stories that incorporate elements of BDSM and power exchange. Please follow me on Amazon, Facebook, or Fetlife if you are interested in updates.

Thank you for your feedback! Your reviews mean so much.

About the Author

LYNNE STEWART is a prolific reader and a lover of all things paranormal and interesting. During the day, she works as a librarian and likes spending time with her husband, their children, and pets. By night, she enjoys creating steamy romances with a little bite in them.

Coming Soon July 2023…

LYNNE STEWART

TEMPTING HIS TRUE MATE

BOOK TWO IN THE
TRUE MATE SHIFTER SERIES

Learn more about Ella and Gabe's story in Tempting his True Mate, Book Two in the True Mate Shifter Series!